BIMINI ROCKS

Atlantis Found?

a novel

by

~ Cheryl Shepherd Bartoszek ~

To Joe, Jarrod and Austin for patient love. Nat, Cynthia, Missy and Raneth for red pen wisdom. To Edie, Shep and Donna for encouragement.

PROLOGUE

"But when the divine element in them became weakened…
and their human traits became predominant, they ceased
to be able to carry their prosperity with moderation."
Plato, *Timaeus* on the people of Atlantis.

Bimini, Bahamas
Present time

Isabelle fidgeted. Her brother, Blue, draped an arm around her tense shoulders.

"Take a deep breath," he said. She obeyed.

"Still not convinced we need to let Zantae in on all this. I mean, I trust her, I do. But sometimes all her crazy talk scares me."

Worry settled on their faces and a knock kept him from responding. He raised an index finger and headed for the door.

"Hold your thought," he said and let Zantae in his apartment.

The native Biminites were charter members of a grass-roots coalition to save Bimini from over development. But this meeting was to share a discovery that could rewrite world history and endanger Bimini worse than any golf course, cruise terminal or hastily built condo.

"Good to see you, Miss Zantae," he said and kissed the wizened lady on her cheek.

She patted his arm and bee-lined to her friend of more than fifty years.

"Hey, Esa, I got all dressed for the meeting and here you two look like you going out to fish," she said as she dropped her hat, purse and sunglasses on the entry table.

Isabelle bristled at the use of her unwanted nickname. Zantae's the only person who gets by with the hated Esa.

"Sit," she ordered.

Blue paced on the other side of the coffee table.

"I found something. Something you've believed in as much as we have." He bent over the coffee table between them, picked up an album and then motioned for the women to scoot over. He sat between them.

"My sister told me about the white lady from Florida, Sirena, who kept having the same underwater dream. Takes place right near the Road to Atlantis."

Isabelle chimed in. "She's not like some tourists or so-called spiritualists who catch Atlantis fever for a day or so. She's hell bent on finding a link to the lost city and Bimini."

Zantae interrupted, "Just say what you know."

"Two, three years ago Sirena tells me a secret. Says she comes here every summer huntin' for the Atlantis link because of a dream so real she can't ignore it. I told my brother."

Zantae put on a sour face, "You violated her confidentiality. And now you're testing my patience. Go on, tell me."

He picked up the conversational ball. "I applied her dream clues to what we know about the reefs near the rocks, the Road to Atlantis."

"Huh, remind me to never tell you a secret," Zantae said in a huff.

He shook his head. "We found proof."

"You going to show me or keep talking?" Zantae folded her arms in exasperation.

He opened a photo album and laid it across Zantae's lap.

She studied a picture of what appeared to be etchings on a wall. Three pyramids. The middle one looked finished and was flanked by two others in various stages of construction. Inside the unfinished pair was a white cylindrical shape, suspended in the center and held vertical with scaffolding. Large basins surrounded the structures.

"Where'd you find this?" Zantae said, eyes glued to the images.

He said, "In a cave, a dry cave. We swam away from the rocks and found a simple coral niche, more of an overhang. We went in and explored until we found an opening, swam through the hole in the ceiling and hit air. The walls are like an art gallery."

Zantae eyed the photo. "This single pyramid provided plenty energy for the islanders. Those other two were constructed because the greedy lords wanted to produce more. The lords insisted the greater pyramid be charged with enough power to outshine the stars. Had to show the enemies we were a force to be reckoned with."

Isabelle held up a palm to stop the monologue. "Gurl, what you mean we were a power? You 'spect us to believe you lived back then?"

Zantae shook her head. "No. What I do 'spect you to believe is I am the keeper of ancient wisdom for the Atlanteans, the Mer Tribe."

"Here we go again with the Mer Tribe," Isabelle said and threw up her hands in disbelief.

Blue intervened. "I believe you are a wisdom keeper. Right now we need your wisdom and guidance."

Isabelle piped up, "Okay, I believe you keep the wisdom, I believe," then added, "You know I'm Christian and don't believe in past lives."

He said, "Well, our great challenge is to validate these findings without putting the world on notice. We need your help."

Zantae held the album to her chest. "A challenge ripe with danger."

~ 1 ~

Day One

Hand scrawled on the side of the beat-up van were the words TAXI MON. Heavy scuba gear bag in tow, I hailed the cab and headed off to my nearby destination, Isabelle's Hideaway. It was mid-July in Bimini, Bahamas and the taxi's air conditioner was on strike. A hot breeze whispered through the casuarina trees but didn't reach me. The window was stuck.

"Hey, Taxi Mon, how do I roll down the window?" I said and pointed a finger downward, "No handle."

"Oh, no problem, ma'am," he said as he lowered the radio volume. He flung an arm over his seat and pointed to the floor. "Find the pliers, yeah. Clamp it to the piece of metal sticking out."

He turned on the overhead light so I could see. I kicked around empty water bottles, a wadded-up pack of rolling papers, spotted, and then excavated a pair of rusty needle-nose pliers from the floorboard. I attached the business end onto the metal nub sticking out of the door and turned about a dozen times. When fresh air breezed in the open window I had to control myself otherwise I'd have stuck my head outside like a puppy. I swayed to the steel drum tunes and begin to transition to sweet island time.

TaxiMon drove me to my home away from home, Isabelle's Hideaway. Pepto pink, the three-story block building situated beside a deep, wide canal stood firm against countless storms. Compared to the islands' newly constructed condos of cheap plywood and slick promises, the Hideaway was a fortress.

The simple ambience of Bimini Island's oldest motel caused my heart to slow and thirst to grow. Over-packed bags in tow, I hauled myself to the lobby slash dining hall slash bar and rang for service.

Judging by the large number of diners seated at tables and elbow benders at the bar, my friend Isabelle made bank on her prime real estate. Throughout the open room people savored the best food on the island, strong adult libations and lively games of billiards. A posse of young girls wiggled around the ever-crooning juke box. I stuck out my lips in disappointment since the charming Isabelle hadn't come out to greet me. Instead, her niece approached me and broke my reverie.

"Hello Miss Sirena, welcome back."

A familiar face beamed at me. Lovely Lonnie, hostess and front desk clerk. I marveled at her beauty. A head taller than my own five eight, her posture indicated total comfort in superior statue and the white, sleeveless dress showed off toned arm muscles. Her smooth, dark complexion fully complemented her wide, contagious smile.

"You've grown into a stunning young lady in one short year."

Lonnie smiled and twirled.

"Thank you."

"So what's new, kiddo?"

"Oh, I'm going to junior year across the pond." She inclined her head eastward. "Jacksonville. Voles Academy swim team recruited me." Lonnie lit another thousand watt smile as she handed over my room key.

"Voles." I let out a low, airy whistle. "Prestigious. Congratulations. Email me your meet schedule. If I can get away from work, I'll come watch and be your biggest cheerleader. By the way, where's my cheerleader, Auntie Isabelle?"

Lonnie giggled. "Oh, she was here till a bit ago. Your plane was so late, she went home to her company. House full of relations. No worries, says she'll return in a little." She paused then queried, "Care for your welcome drink now?"

"Bring it to my room?"

Lonnie tossed back her braided locks and shook her head. She strode to the bar and asked the silver-haired barkeep to mix the house special, a stiff Bahama Mama.

Watching him create my drink nearly hypnotized me. He juggled bottles and threw in some fancy hand work. Mesmerized, I went into deep thought on why I came here during hurricane season. The whole trip got off to a bad start. My plane was delayed, the flight from Lauderdale to South Bimini was turbulent as hell and my best island buddy wasn't here.

Lonnie called my name and wiggled a forefinger.

"Miss Sirena, I said, you are not hiding upstairs, move yourself to here," she patted a high backed swivel stool.

Shoulders slumped, I stomped away from my pile of belongings. I could never refuse Lonnie, especially with her beautiful Bahamian lilt.

"Now. Soak in some of this fine Biminite charm."

Orange glistened through the clear tumbler. I took a short

pull on the skinny straw. If I consume more than two of these concoctions, alcohol poisoning's a bloated promise.

"Remind me. Just how many types of rum does this involve? Ten?"

Lonnie's face smiled. Her blue eyes danced. "No, only four. Coconut, two dark rums and one secret weapon. Oh and a splash of OJ."

"Keyword splash," I said and warned, "Prepare to carry me and my stuff upstairs."

"You, no," Lonnie winked. "Your belongings, yes." She sashayed back to the hostess stand.

The welcome drink went down like hot silk. Action at the bar included a younger set of locals playing ring the hook while a trio of middle-aged men engaged in a serious billiards game. An older generation graced the bar next to a few loud and happy white tourists. They looked and sounded American. Fishermen, not golfers.

"Care for another?" the barkeep asked.

I nodded, already glassy-eyed.

He delivered my drink and I got a better look at him.

"Hey, aren't you Percy?"

"Yes, and you are Sirena. Wondered if you'd remember."

"Welcome back." He winked.

A woman walked over and sat by me, the only empty seat. She wasted no time in ordering a Kalik Gold, Bahama's national beer.

"Hey, nice t-shirt," she said to me. "Weeki Wachee, the mermaid place. I went there when I was a kid. So you been there, too?"

I paused a couple seconds. "You might say that." And paused a few more.

She looked at me and her face urged me to continue. "I live there."

"How crazy to live by mermaids. Ever meet any?"

"You're talking to one."

"Get out!" Her brown eyes bugged. "For real?" She took a long sip of brew. "What prompted you to take the plunge?" She giggled at her own joke.

I rolled my eyes and started looking for Lonnie, to get me out of here and into my quiet room.

The chatty tourist pursed her already plump lips. "Wow is all I can muster. Wow. Wow. Wow." She looked at my hand and touched my silvery wedding band.

"Where's your husband? Is he a merman?" she giggled and looked around.

"Somethin' like that. He passed a few years ago."

"I took a beautiful story and messed it up. I am so sorry." She looked up and sighed. "Since we're both flying solo, if you think you can stand me, let's do a dive together. I assume you're here to dive. And maybe hit Alice Town one night."

I nodded. "We'll see." I said but didn't mean it.

It was difficult to tune out her high pitched jabber, something about a cheating boyfriend. I feigned interest and scouted around for Lonnie. I needed rescuing.

"I'm Jane. From Hollywood." she said and added, "California." She raised her empty beer bottle. We toasted to mermaids and divers. I told her my name and she raised an eyebrow. Before she could joke about Sirena and the mermaid implication, I ordered her another beer.

"Hey, you're diving from Isabelle's boat, right?"

I nodded. Dear Lord when is she gonna shut up, I thought.

"Last time I was here five years ago, some real freaky types were on the boat with me. Spiritualists doing underwater meditating or something. At Bimini Road, the rocks. Anyway, you must've dived the rocks."

I shrugged, "It's what I live for."

She cocked her head to the side, shiny brown hair falling over a shoulder. "What's your take on it? Roadbed or harbor?" She took a breath. "Or some natural formation, just happens to look man made."

"I guess it's whatever we make of it."

"Well, I plan on taking a ton of pics." She glanced at her Rolex Mariner. "Going to my room. I'm on the early boat. You?"

"Nope."

She walked off and waved. I looked at my trusty Freestyle dive watch. Getting late.

Lonnie checked in another late arrival and then turned her attention to me. "You doing all right?"

"Will you order me a fried fish platter with beans and rice? Have it sent up, please ma'am. Oh, and can I steal you a sec? Need a little assist with drink and all."

"No problem."

Lonnie led the way upstairs. She wore my overstuffed backpack and toted the dangerous elixir. I prayed we wouldn't pass by smokers in the hall. Volatile rocket fuel came to mind as I managed to pull my bag up every step and to the one-and-a-half star room.

Lonnie turned to me. "Why're you here so late?"

"The little Otter needed a brake job in Melbourne, where I got on, so we had to wait a couple hours. Then in Lauderdale we picked up two passengers and had to wait some more for a storm to pass. Still hit some good turbulence, though."

Lonnie's eyes showed concern then relief. "You're here now. Safe with us. Safe on the ground."

"Ahh the storm was a hefty reminder. The merry month of May is far preferable to the tropical storm-prone July. This is my first and last July pilgrimage to your fair isle."

She dropped the suitcases with a bang and then stuck out her hand, I dug the key from my skirt pocket and plopped it in her eager hand. She unlocked, flipped on the room light, overhead fan and passed my drink.

"Thanks," I said. "You still first mate on Auntie's charter boat?" I fished out a couple of bills and gave them to her. She thanked me and pointed to the key on the table.

"Occasionally. Might work tomorrow afternoon's charter. You going morning or afternoon?"

"Not morning. If you don't minding checking, I'd like to be on the afternoon manifest."

She flashed the hand signal for okay and shut the garish gold door behind her. I ripped off my torture bra without even loosening my t-shirt.

The dangerous drink parched my throat. Of course tourists aren't supposed to consume tap water so I'd need to get a pitcher of filtered water real soon.

A quarter hour later there was a knock. Maybe Lonnie's back with water. I opened up to Isabelle, who gracefully balanced a loaded food tray.

"Don't expect a tip," I deadpanned.

"Then don't expect the food," she teased and half turned to leave.

I relieved her of the tray and set it down on the scratched Formica table for two.

"Well, here I am." We hugged, held hands and then looked at each other from arms' lengths. I added, "Just in time to do the silly storm dance."

We twisted and snickered like school girls. She'd barely aged. Skin almost smooth as Lonnie's. Once I commented on her gorgeous complexion and she'd quipped, "You know black don't crack."

She relaxed in the wicker chair. I plopped in the plastic one next to the table, and started to unwrap my food. "So. Spill all the coconut telegraph news." I took a bite of fish and purred with satisfaction. Nobody could cook like Isabelle's hand-picked staff.

She didn't answer right away. Her expression was one usually reserved for Sunday confessions. "First I say the bad news." She took a deep breath, walked to the table, and poured us each a shot of the spiced rum she brought. She threw it back and made a teary sigh. I waved off my proffered tot. She held it up to the overhead light studying the rum as if reading tea leaves.

"Trouble in paradise. Marina at casino on North Bimini fixin' to dredge and build a crazy long dock on the west side. For the go-fast mini-cruise ships." She put the tot on the table.

"You are kidding. Bimini Rocks and all the near shore reefs could smother under a ton of silt and crap."

She nodded. Her head full of soft gray curls rocked in agreement. "Gull, it so bad. Nobody listens to Biminites. They got answers to everything you say and den some. We got a coalition, Save Bimini, they spoke to the Ministry of Tourism, went to Nassau, spoke against dredging at the special hearing. But marina's got deep pockets and gov'ment tired of Biminites, the young uns, leaving home to find work."

"Bull. Shit." I emphasized each syllable.

"In a week, maybe sooner, the dredging begins."

"Who can condone dredging?" I leaned back in my chair.

"All the Biminites thought it would get stopped. Never dreamed this could happen to our home, our sea." She tossed back another shot. "Tomorrow we talk more about the dredging devils. For now I tell the good news. You have a dive buddy for the whole month. My brother from Florida."

"James." I always dived with James.

"No. James comes in May. This time you get Blue. Lonnie's daddy."

"Not sauntering Blue." I was too tired to be angry.

She cracked a smile.

"He got a bad rap. That boy shy and he a geek." She flipped a wrist at the air and me.

Leaning forward, I grabbed the fork and air hammered it toward her.

"Spill the news worth me coming here in hurricane season."

She raised an index finger and then her glass. We clinked

and then chugged. Ah, the soothing burn, the yin and yang of good alcohol. I flopped on the bed, satisfied.

"So," she said, settling back down. "First we talk about my brother. Stop giving me the hoo doo eye," she shook a fore-finger as if scolding a naughty child. "He gonna help you find something on Bimini Rocks before you get too old to dive."

~2~

Day One

Isabelle picked up the half-empty bottle of rum and looked over her glass at me. Raising a hand to wave her off I said, "No way. Besides, didn't you just insult me?"

She chuckled, stood and meandered to the table. "Just sayin' what true. You fifty, yes?"

I nodded and swung my legs from soft bed to tiled floor. My head spun. "And you got me snockered. Again."

She moved her shoulders up and down in a silent chuckle. After pouring me a glass of cool water she gathered up dirty dishes and stuck them on the tray.

"Take the rocket fuel with you," I said.

She looked up from tightening the rum lid, lay the bottle on the tray, hoisted it and headed for the door. "Got it. And you on tomorrow's afternoon charter.

"I'm not too old to dive?"

"I'll let ya know."

I stumbled over to open the door. She beat me to it.

I asked, "You working in the morning?"

"No. Late shift. Sweet dreams." She disappeared into the heavy night.

"Ditto."

I fell across the bed in gritty street clothes. Sleep took me like a thief.

Vivid colors swirled and gave me a sense of slowly sinking, twirling under water. Aquamarine to silky azure melted to stunning turquoise. I joined a stunning school of animated looking parrot fish, we swam over coral and sea fans. The familiar scene bathed me in dappled watercolors exquisite as stained glass. From my peripheral I spied a massive fish tail. I spun around and caught a glimpse of a merman. My scaly companions scattered. I pursued the descending tail, kicked hard to catch up. I chased him over Bimini Road. He swam into a cavern.

● ● ●

Day Two

A piercing, obnoxious sound exploded in my ears. I swallowed and choked, no longer able to breathe underwater. My dream evaporated. Again.

"What the…" I peeled myself off the ceiling. As the neighbor's alarm was silenced, another noise assaulted my ears. A shrill, off-key voice spewed curse words through the motel's thin walls. Pillow over my face, I tried to drift back into the recurring dream, the ethereal vision of Bimini Road forever ending on a premature note. I gave up, opened my weary eyes and experienced a dream and a rum hangover, both in serious competition with loud hunger pangs.

Sporadic cursing continued from outside. "Bitch, bitch, bitch."

I flung open the window and peered into the predawn void, poised to curse the curser. The faded, cracked walkway below my window looked empty. I shrugged to myself and headed to the bathroom to brush my furry teeth. Somehow I managed to pull most of my tangled red curls off my face. I lassoed the thick pony tail with a heavy duty Rastafarian hued hair tie.

Famished, I shot downstairs and followed my freckled nose to the sumptuous aroma of coffee.

"Morning," said a chipper guy behind the breakfast bar.

"Morning. What time is it?" I stammered and helped myself to a cup of joe from the samovar. I tried to focus on the face of my watch. Man I was in bad shape.

"Nearly six," he said.

I embraced the coffee cup and slurped hot comfort. Other breakfast aromas teased as a loud stomach growl betrayed me. Sliding sideways onto a bar stool, I made a point to avoid eye contact with the cheerful man.

From the corner of my eye I saw him nod. "You must be Sirena. I'm Blue."

His sexy Bahamian lilt irritated me. Pretending to focus on coffee, I cut my eyes hard to the side. "Yep." I slurped some more.

He nodded his head as he finished drying a stemmed glass and slid it in an overhead rack. He welcomed tourists and locals as they filed into the Hideaway, eager for coffee, breakfast and gossip.

An intense feeling of déjà vu tugged at me. I shook off the physical exclamation points being too hung over to care. I lowered the cup and stared into space. A voice halted my rambling thoughts.

"Sirena?"

"Huh, yes?"

My clothes were slept-in, hair wiry as seaweed, and my eyes resembled green olives in a bloody Mary. I set down the brew, hoping he'd keep his sexy eyes away from me.

"You diving this morning?" He asked.

"No. I'm the afternoon delight," I barbed. Then wished I hadn't.

He belly laughed. People stared.

"Isabelle said you had a dry wit."

"What else did she tell you?" I twisted a stray tendril around my finger, sizing up Isabelle's kid brother.

"You have a good heart but are a bit of a toasted marshmallow."

Not surprised, I swung around to face him eyeball to eyeball. He offered a hand. I took it and we shook hands for long seconds. Above his perfectly chiseled nose were, God help me, robin's egg blue eyes, my weakness. We dropped hands.

"You sorry you signed on to be my dive guide?"

His face lit up. "Not a t' all."

"Your sister says you have something important to tell me." I opened my eyes wide and tilted my head to one side.

"Ah yes. We're buddies for the month, for all the afternoon delights."

My face grew warm.

"She hinted there was some news. About Atlantis?"

He made the so-so sign with his hands. "It's complicated."

"Brother, you don't have a clue about complications. I'm starting to feel like ya'll got me over here under false pretenses."

He flushed. "Not true. There's more to know, to share. And we shall. Just," he looked around, "not this moment."

"Well, if it's not too complicated, do you think you can get my breakfast tray? Coupla muffins, three slices of real bacon and a pitcher of cold water?" I emphasized the words, "To go."

"Of course." He jotted my order and rang a hand bell. A server picked up the order and disappeared to the kitchen. "Slice of mango to tide you over?"

He dishes a peace offering after I insult him. I smiled a little, nodded my thanks and then refilled my mug before I devoured the sweet juicy mango.

Breakfast was delivered quickly and I balanced the tray toward the outside stairwell. The heat hit me and I cursed myself for not staying at the breakfast counter. I managed to make it to the third floor deck. Sunrise painted the sky and pained my eyes. Caffeine and food helped arrest the twin jackhammers in my head. I frisked myself. Man, I could use my sunglasses.

Sugar level and attitude adjusted, I ambled to my room and shucked out of sticky, wrinkled clothes. A shower further elevated my mood and I forgave Isabelle for the hook up attempt.

Year after year I pilgrim to Bimini in May like a sea turtle making her nest. She must have something monumental to share about Atlantis. Otherwise she wouldn't have insisted I drag my ass out here during storm season. Years ago I first jumped off a dive boat with my husband Sterling and we plunged over The Road to Atlantis, the local dive site known as Bimini Rocks. First time on the island all I cared about was logging as many dives as possible in the aquamarine sea. The boat captain briefed us on his Atlantis theory and said the massive rocks of The Road could have been set by Atlanteans prior to 10,000 BC.

Our dive along the rocks was the last time Sterling and I dived together.

He badgered me in a silly way to join his adventures. Our common denominator was diving but he yearned for more. Motocross cycling and rappelling both were hobbies he initiated and I endured. My passion was the water.

Skydiving was on his bucket list and I refused to rubber stamp it on mine. After he tandemed the required number of jumps, he ventured into solo diving. I couldn't bear to watch the video when he was safely on land. It became his male bonding hobby. He and three guy friends went to Mexico to skydive by the Sea of Cortez. Their wives and I tagged along for the pristine scuba diving. We were underwater when the accident unfolded.

Day Two

After the morning jumps, Sterling's buds sped off in a new Range Rover to their modern hotel while Sterling hopped in a big-tired open jeep. He headed to our place, a charming casita by the sea. He got stuck behind a pickup on a dusty Mexican road. Something flew from the truck bed. Sterling swerved, went off-road and slammed into a tree. Losing him to the sky or the sea, would've seemed like pure destiny. Losing him to a rusty bucket flying from a pickup truck was worse than torture.

I threw myself in work. Work takes me from coast to coast with gigs in aquariums, fresh water springs, private and special events.

My first experience wagging a mermaid tail was at a Florida attraction at the ripe age of 15 years. My mother worked as a janitor there. The mermaids adopted me and I was somewhat of a mascot who got to dress up and follow the performers around during practice. I became a hell of a breath holder.

Back then, training lasted until the head mermaid gave the new minnow a nod. It took me 18 months to master skills and win over the boss.

● ● ●

Preparing for my afternoon dive, I stepped into a green one-piece swim suit and then braided the majority of my wild hair into a couple of low pigtails. With half an hour to kill before boarding, I flopped on the bed and pored over my trusty dive log.

After logging more than 200 dives along the Road to Atlantis and going over scores of research documents, I was convinced the rocks weren't a natural occurrence. On the other hand, my dream was no more scientific than the feeling in my gut. The gut feeling cost me a month of vacation time and a big bite out of my earnings every summer.

After Sterling died, those dreams morphed into nightly recurrences. Atlantis became real to me and my curiosity escalated to a full-blown obsession.

If I figure out where the recurring dream takes place I know I'll find the big "X" on the treasure map, a piece of the Lost City of Atlantis. But there's no map or local knowledge of an undersea cavern anywhere near Bimini Road. Closest I've found are erosion caverns out by Turtle Cay.

Once again I flipped through my tattered log book hoping to come across some missed clue. I lingered over snap shots of the rocks which create Bimini Road. Dog-eared entries caught my attention but nothing jumped out. At half past eleven it was time to motivate to the dive boat.

Blue was onboard his sister's charter boat, *Sweet Pea,* chatting with Lonnie. Successful businesses are a family affair on Bimini Isle. I fetched my heavy gear bag from the downstairs shed where I'd stashed it this morning and headed toward the boat. Halfway between the dock and the shed, I paused a couple seconds to check out Blue whose deep brown skin reflected his proud Biminite heritage. He was a tall man, maybe six-six. I started walking again and thought of Lonnie, his spitting image except for one difference. She had one eye green and the other blue.

Her Auntie said she starting wearing a contact over the green one, to cover her mother's unwanted gene.

Almost to the boat under the hot, proud sun, it was 95 in the shade and I was moving slow mo. The captain spotted me and waved.

"Welcome back," the captain said.

I waved back. "Hey. Great to see ya, El Cap. Looks like a perfect day to dive."

Once on board I dropped my gear bag. A floppy hat and oversized sunglasses nearly obscured my face. My fair complexion was slathered in sun block, making me look like a real tourist. I stood next to El Cap and we both gazed at the flat horizon of the emerald sea.

"How's my favorite Florida girl?"

I opened my arms and gave him a hug.

"You got a buddy today?"

"What if I don't?" He released me and simultaneously wagged a forefinger. He made a tsk-tsk sound to indicate he wouldn't allow any solo divers.

I pointed to Blue. My body language yelled, 'As if you don't know already.'

He grinned and then moved on to chat with other passengers. I reached out and grabbed Lonnie by her wasp waist. She yanked one of my pigtails.

"Two jobs. When do you practice?" I asked.

Lonnie pulled me closer, smiling. "Glad you could make it this afternoon, Sleeping Beauty." A dark expression consumed her. "Ah, Mother Mary Grace arranged for me to work out early mornings at the casino marina's pool." She and her mother got along like a snake and a mongoose.

I gauged my fellow passengers. The manifest consisted of a small group of New Jersey dive club members, wearing identical t-shirts, plus a young couple who couldn't keep their paws off each other.

A Jersey guy said, "We doing the rocks first?"

El Cap nodded.

"Okay. Let's do the floating bordello for our second dive," Jersey boy said with a snicker.

Gimme a break, I thought and rolled my shaded eyes.

"So it is," El Cap said. He climbed the ladder to the bridge and cranked the twin diesels to a purr.

Lonnie untied lines from the dock and shoved off. The vessel floated in canal water tinted a deep emerald. High noon and the blistering sun's wattage amplified the surreal blue sky.

Blue motioned for me to sit by him. I hauled my gear bags over and sat next to him in the shade. Soothed by the engine hum, heady from the perfume of diesel and brine, my afternoon delight was underway.

With practiced hands, we each assembled our gear. I slid on and secured onto a small air tank a buoyancy compensator. Worn vest-like, the BC held or expelled air with the push of a button. Air in to go up, dump air to sink. The regulator delivered breathing air. I opened the tank's valve and read the air pressure gauge, a hair over 3000 psi. Perfect. The BC's inflator hose worked and the computer with depth gauge was alive and ready. I opened my camera bag, took the little GoPro from its wide angle housing, turned it on and fiddled with settings. We had a few minutes to go before gearing up at the rocks.

He broke the ice. "So, how long you been diving?"

"Isabelle didn't tell you?" I looked up from my task.

"If she had I wouldn't ask."

"Come on. Half the island knows I'm a mermaid actress." He looked sheepish. "Got me. I know you're a mermaid. That's not exactly diving."

"Excuse me. Let me throw your happy ass overboard, legs bound, no mask, and you grasp around for a skinny breathing tube. Execute perfectly synchronized dances with three other performers for forty minutes in seventy-two degree water. No wetsuit."

"Fair." He studied his flip flops.

"To answer your question, started mermaid school when I was 15 and got an advanced dive cert much later, with my late husband."

"I'm sorry for your loss."

I nodded a thank you. "So many years. Seems like yesterday. Seems like forever." I dropped the camera in my dry bag. "Look, you know I'm hell bent on proving an Atlantean city was here. Isabelle insisted July was the time to hunt for it and hinted she had some clues to share with me. Yet you two aren't being straight with me. Why?" I looked at my reflection in his mirrored aviators.

"Isabelle said you needed a seasoned tour guide. She's tired of seeing you spin your fins."

"Spin my fins?" I was about ready to spin my head, backwards a la Exorcist. I shook my head and fished around in the camera bag for the extension pole.

"As your personal guide, it is my duty to insure you have a more than satisfactory dive. What is your objective today, Sirena?" He delivered this in an upbeat, tour guide, American sounding voice. Good thing I forgot the pole, or I'd have bopped him upside his ridiculous head.

"Cut the crap. You know." I peered at him over the top of my fake tortoise shell shades then added, "My gut says there's something in or around those rocks to link Bimini to the people of Atlantis." I twisted my silver octopus bracelet round and round my wrist. "But you know that, don't you?"

Before he could look up from twiddling his thumbs, Lonnie announced, "Five minutes." She walked over to her father and said, "Wish I could dive with you today, Papa."

"How about tomorrow?" he said.

She gave him the okay sign and turned to assist other passengers with their gear.

"By the way, Mr. 'I'm your tour guide', you haven't bothered to listen to my dive plan. What happened to plan the dive, dive the plan?"

I marched over and stuck the tiny camera in its housing, dropped it in my BC pocket, stashed the hat and glasses in a dry bag and picked up my wetsuit. As I shrugged into the super thin nylon suit, I wondered what the hell Isabelle had up her apron sleeve. At the moment I wanted to fire her little brother's sassy ass.

The boats' twin Cat diesels powered down. Water sloshed.

People chatted. Up above, the winged beggars known as sea gulls squealed for hand-outs.

"Tell me your plan. Then after everyone else is safely in the water, I'll tell you what we're really going to do." He didn't look at me as he shouldered into his BC and buckled it around his naked torso.

I exhaled deeply. "Those rocks, the road, I see more than boulders lined up in sand. And I feel more than the warm water around me." I paused then added, "So I'm gonna trust you are here to help me stop spinning my fins."

"Fair."

From the bow, Lonnie affixed a line to a mooring line and ball instead of dropping anchor. It better protected the reef, rocks and aquatic growth from clumsy anchors. I stood and focused on the sea, clear enough to spy yellowtail snapper darting under and around the boat, a classic 46-foot Newton.

A gusty breeze gave me a shiver. Blue stepped over and touched my shoulders to get my attention. "You may need more than a one mil." He pulled my wetsuit sleeve out. When he let go, it popped my skin. His playful gestures were a warm distraction. I rubbed my arm.

"I'm fine."

El Cap was at the stern in front of the aluminum dive platform. "Everyone have a buddy?"

Each passenger pointed to their respective buddy. Blue pointed to himself then me. He rapped his knuckles on the small sixty-three cubic foot air tank.

"Your air consumption must be impressive." He eyed me in an off-handed way.

"Like a mermaid."

"Indeed. We'll let the others go first."

So, I'll get the dive plan in bits and pieces. Lovely.

He double-checked his gear. I did the same and then chugged water as we awaited El Cap's briefing.

I'd heard the captain's long-winded mini-lectures since the first day he stepped foot on this boat. He'd crewed or captained for Isabelle more than three years. Mid-twenties, his shoulder-length straight hair was streaked bronze courtesy of salt and sun. Tethered sunglasses dangled from his neck. His golden brown eyes were set in a large, square face. His open shirt, stark white shorts and Greek captain hat added to his air of utter confidence.

Arms akimbo and slightly swaying on sea legs dark and stout as mahogany, the captain addressed his passengers.

"Basically you believe in Atlantis. Or not," he said in a sing-song accent. "Plato wrote in 360 BC of highly advanced, spiritual people who discovered and populated Atlantis. I interpret this as a historical account. The small continent disappeared some twelve thousand years ago, most likely annihilated by undersea volcano eruptions or another powerful energy source." He paced before the captive audience.

"We Biminites respect this mysterious yet sacred site. As you shall see, the rocks along the sandy bottom are fitted into a placement pattern, right angles, far too orderly to have simply come from nature." He paused long enough for his passengers to look at each other and whisper.

"Some liken the rocks to similar roads running across the floor of the Yucatan. These rocks are in pairs, hundreds of them, in three to four meters, oh, about ten to twelve feet deep. They stretch on for a half mile, make a hook curve then disappear beneath the sand."

Dead silence aboard. Only water lapping against the boat and persistent gulls dare utter sounds.

"Go port side, he points to the left. Snorkel on the water surface until you get a visual on the rocks and drop down."

Fidgety and hot after the long-winded Captain, the other divers' eager faces signaled they were beyond jazzed and ready to go. But El Cap wasn't quite finished with his captives.

"Current is stiff today so stay in this general vicinity, do not venture behind the boat until ready to come aboard. Remember to return with at least 500 pounds of air. And one more thought. No souvenirs. Take only photos. Leave only bubbles. Pool's open!"

We all stood in our cumbersome gear. Lonnie and El Cap assisted each person as they waddled toward the dive platform, heavy with gear and awkward from finned feet.

A flying fish launched itself airborne as if on cue to get this party hopping.

"I'm usually first in, last out and today I want to sweep east-west across the rocks, not up and down, twenty minutes max. Then head to the reef outcroppings. I'm looking for..."

He shook his head no and interrupted. "We'll do a negative entry. Drift behind the boat to the next mooring ball. Drop down and hang onto the chain if the current's strong. At the bottom, look for a chimney-type protrusion. The compass will become a little jittery since it's some sort of an energy source."

"Whoa, whoa, El Cap specifically says...energy source?"

He nodded. "After the chimney, we'll go east until we see a cavern opening."

"Cavern?" He uttered the magic word. Elevated heartbeats thudded out of my wetsuit.

"Notice El Cap keeps his divers ahead of the boat. Besides today's slight current, it's to keep them strictly on the rocks." He un-velcroed then dropped a small flashlight in my BC pocket on top of the camera.

For once I was speechless. Cavern.

I spit onto my face plate, rubbed the spittle around to defog the tempered glass and dipped it in the rinse bucket on my way down to the dive platform.

Last ones off, we did giant strides into the water and another dimension. I dropped like a stone, easily clearing my ears. Instead of pausing to take in the seascape, I followed the leader all the way to the chimney. He's right, the compass needle was jittery. So was I. Cavern's gotta be next, I repeated in my mind as I pulled out and donned gloves, palmed the camera and clicked away.

Peering down the three foot tall protrusion, it seemed bottomless. Sea fans swayed on top of the chimney. I pulled out the light and after a few failed attempts, it clicked on. Tiny cobalt fishes swam carefree, darting from side-to-side in the gray sponge-like opening. Was this an ancient chimney for smoke to escape or a well to tap fresh water? I snapped a few stills, slid the light's lanyard over my wrist, changed setting from photo to video and used the flashlight as a crude modeling light.

He motioned to follow him onward. I turned the camera off and slipped it up my wetsuit sleeve. We swam over the top of a ledge. Twirling an index finger, he signaled to turn around. He swam back and beneath a ten-foot wide, six-foot tall ledge. It's the kind nurse sharks favor as a resting crib. Close on his fins, I glanced back and took a quick compass reading, needle now steady. I had the numbers for our way out and had a hair over 2800 pounds of air. Depth gauge indicated twenty feet, and we'd been down fifteen minutes. I looked up. The cavern. My heart and stomach turned somersaults.

He swam to the very back of the gray colored overhang. Pointing the light beams up, we swam in clear water toward the orange and yellow sponge-encrusted ceiling.

Hand-over-hand he touched the ceiling until his forearm disappeared into a void. We made eye contact. He pointed upward then kicked through and disappeared. I swallowed hard and followed through the equivalent of an attic door. He tied a long yellow line to a piece of coral. At the end of the line dangled a Cyalume glow stick.

We pulled our gear-laden selves up to a partially submerged shelf and maneuvered to sitting positions. Our hips in water but dry from waist up and immersed in darkness except for our artificial lights. Blue slid his mask below his chin. So did I.

The *Twilight Zone* tune resonated in my head. Lapping water created a gentle percussion. Each sound we generated echo-amplified in the eerie abyss, including my heartbeats. Our finned feet dangled in the salt water, over the escape hatch. The air smelled like stale seaweed and fish.

My hands shook as we cross-checked our pressure gauges. "We both have plenty of air. Still, we'll only stay a few minutes," he said. The depth gauge read eleven feet.

When I found my voice I said, "Dear God, this is my dream. How long have you known about this? Who else knows?" A tear drop rolled from my face into the sea.

He painted the walls with a powerful light beam. I did the same. The cave reminded me of the inside of a tepee. We sat on a skinny rock plateau surrounded by sloping walls too far away to touch. The areas closest to the waterline were embedded with what appeared to be dimensional wallpaper of sea biscuits and sand dollars.

My light beam stroked the wall furthest from us and illuminated markings. "Graffiti?" I asked, directing the beam to get a better look.

"No. Art. From the Lost City."

"Atlantis. Art?"

"Most likely from that era." He tried to shed light on the ceiling. "Hard to see all the stars painted across the ceiling."

I marveled at the sight, the suggestion, the culmination of my dream.

"A sample I submitted to a trusted colleague, an art historian at the University of Miami, dated this to around 12,000 BC."

"I have studied," he stopped mid-sentence to say, "Listen."

Rumbling sounds reverberated and struck a chord in my bones. We locked eyes and didn't waste time in donning our masks. We torpedoed through the passageway where the lit Cyalume line hung. Scrambling, we moved high speed out of the cave. I dumped my BC of excess air, and plummeted, striking the sea floor with enough force to jar my teeth. I was almost clear of the cavern. I pushed off the bottom and kicked forward but was tugged to a halt. He swam in open water a couple of body lengths ahead. I tried to back up. Stuck. Moved to the left then right. Stuck. The spare regulator and hose tightly wedged on something out of my reach. Damn purge button depressed, and my precious air hissed from the octopus regulator, burning fast.

~4~

Day Two

As silver dollar size coral and limestone fell from the cavern's ceiling, I planted my body on the sea floor and threw my arms over my head. My tank vibrated from hits by the crumbling ceiling.

Waist down, I was under the cavern, waist up, nothing but the sea above.

Pinned to the seafloor like a weak wrestler in a lopsided match, I had to take action as soon as the pelting ceased. Attempting to shrug out of my BC, which held air tank and weight pouches, another problem arose, a buckle snagged. No matter how hard I tried to unbuckle the chest strap, the plastic piece of shit wouldn't open. I reached for my knife, always mounted on the front of my BC. Empty. No knives allowed on the Bimini Road dive, too many souvenirs were taken and fools carved their initials in the stones. El Cap had collected and stashed all knives before we donned our gear.

After what seemed like an eternity, he power-finned back. Miming are you okay, I gave the hand signal for so-so, and made a face causing water to seep inside my face mask. I cleared it as he checked my air gauge and put his left wrist in front of my face. He tapped his right forefinger on his wrist then flashed all five fingers, meaning 1500 pounds of air was in my tank. He

kicked up a sandy cloud. I could feel him tug on the spare regulator hose. He came back, facemask to facemask, then motioned
for me to back up. I did and it put some slack on the hose. He
darted back to the regulator. Several attempts to dislodge the
snared regulator failed. He came back around and motioned for
me to remove my BC. It also held air tank and weights. I shook
my head no, pointed to the buckle and gave it the middle finger.

I pointed to my empty knife sheath and aped a back and
forth saw motion with my hands then pointed behind me. He
shook his head no. I saw his big-ass knife sheathed on his leg
and pointed to it. Cut the damn coral, I tried to communicate,
again motioning like a saw with my hand. He violently shook
his head no. Since he couldn't man-up and cut a bit of coral,
he's gonna owe me at least a grand in equipment.

He came at me with the eight-inch knife and cut the buckle
strap. I unbuckled the cummerbund and then shrugged out of
my gear. I straddled the BC wrapped tank, willing my fins to
stay on the bottom. I glanced back at the pinned hose and reg.
It wasn't tangled in a piece of pretty coral growing from the sea
bed. A boulder size hunk of stone had landed on the regulator
hose. Any closer and my next gear purchase would've been a
prosthesis flipper. Or a tombstone.

I hung onto my tank to keep from making a fast and poten-
tially deadly uncontrolled ascent. Biting the regulator mouthpiece so hard my jaws ached, I concentrated on breath control.
Good lord, I'm chomping at the proverbial bit and I breath hold
for a living.

Blue's arms encircled my ribcage. He pulled my body in
front of his to control my positive buoyancy. I released the tank,

slowed my breath and then released the reg, blowing exhalation bubbles until he fed me his spare regulator. Its long yellow hose wrapped around him and fit between my lips. I clamped down on the mouthpiece, exhaled to purge water, then drew a deep breath. We made a slow ascent. He gave the okay signal in front of my mask. I returned it over my shoulder. We kept our controlled pace. I synchronized my kicks to his, cocooned in his bare arms.

We rose toward our world of air where rain drops tattooed the water surface. Surreal beauty, yet a grim reminder we're mere visitors. An unwelcome one today, it seems.

I spit out his regulator and floated from his arms. He gripped my hand, inflated his BC then dropped the reg from his mouth.

"What took you so long?"

"You're welcome."

I stuttered, "The cave, the art. Was that a quake?" I hollered. "My ears are ringing like a yoga gong." And my head ached. The sight of a boulder on my gear, fractions from my leg made me ill.

He nodded. "Could be a slight tremor," he said, still holding my hand.

"Good Lord."

"But really more like a blast," he added.

"I can barely hear you. Did you say a blast? Like dynamite?" My words were muffled although I knew I was yelling.

He nodded and let go of me long enough to inflate a four-foot long bright orange emergency sausage. I spotted and pointed out the dive boat, a quarter mile or so away. We each put a fist atop our heads, international diver signal to the boat crew meaning I'm okay.

"You found the cave. I knew I wasn't crazy." I rubbed my head then checked my hand for blood. None. Something bumped my bottom.

"Hey, did you just goose me?" I quelled the urge to back hand him.

"What do you mean, goose?"

I checked him out. Both his hands were above water. Great. Now I got a shark checking me out.

"It's a turtle. Right behind you."

He pivoted and gave a chuckle. "Hum, it's ole One Eye. Been trying to grab him the last couple days. He's picked up a nasty piece of trash on a flipper. Needs to be excised before it grows in his skin."

Ole One Eye swam right up to me, eyeballs to eyeball. His right eye was gone and there was a plastic six pack holder shoved up his left flipper like an evil bangle bracelet. I put an arm around his shell behind his head, held the big beast as Blue grabbed at the plastic trash. Two hard yanks and it came off. My wetsuit protected the inside of my forearms from his barnacles.

One Eye exhaled through his nostrils, closed them off and sank. He goosed me again on his way down.

"Hey!" I hollered and grabbed my derriere. Insult on top of injuries.

"Ha. Old boy's got a crush on you."

The boat motored toward us through waves that had picked up since our descent. I bobbed on the surface like a floating coconut and we held hands to keep from being separated. The rumbling diesel motor grew louder, fumes mingled with the iodine scent of the sea. The big boat eased next to us and El Cap shifted the boat props to neutral.

Lonnie shouted, "Papa, are you okay?" She would have jumped in if El Cap hadn't put a gentle hand on her. Shaking, she helped us up the platform to our seating area.

"Oh buoy. What's become of your gear?" Lonnie asked, ashen faced.

"I can explain later. Let's get back to the dock." He drew his daughter close to his chest.

"Thank you," I said. Seeing Lonnie slapped me into reality. I draped my trembling arms around Blue and his precious girl.

"More than welcome." We group hugged for a few sweet seconds. His daughter steadied his tank from the bottom, a valiant attempt to ease the gear's weight off her father. With both hands on the tank boot, she trailed him as he waddled to a bench, sat and removed his gear.

Lonnie grabbed a clipboard and called roll. When she was positive everyone was present and accounted for, she gave the waiting captain an okay signal. I felt all eyes on me, the gearless one.

El Cap addressed his frightened passengers. "Like I said before, I think we experienced an earthquake. But the expert on board is Doctor Rolle, a geologist who may have a thing or two to say about today's event."

I reeled from his words. Far more than a dive guide and aficionado of Atlantis, El Cap said he's a professor at Florida Institute of Technology. And he found the cave. My cave. With art.

I peeled out of my wetsuit and cursed. Shit for brains left her camera in the abandoned BC. I wanted to heave overboard and rescue my camera. But I just sat. A sense of loss overcame me and the Hebrew phrase Sit Shiva came to mind.

Dr. Rolle stood and addressed us. "Slight tremors typically generate no aftershocks or tsunamis for North or South Bimini since we are on the Blake Plateau and protected from tidal waves."

One of the Jersey guys stood. "It's gotta be more than that. My freakin' ears are ringing like St. Stephens Cathedral." He jerked his head toward his left shoulder a bunch of times then repeated the action on his right, attempting to get water, or sound, from his ears. "And Chrissake why did she ditch her gear?" He pointed at me.

El Cap bellowed, "She is alive and well. Our main concern. Now, Doctor, you were saying?" El Cap had directed his loud words and steely stare at Jersey boy, who slowly sat back in his seat.

Blue fumbled with his sunglasses before sliding them over his eyes. "Yes. It could have been something else, but, as I said, I won't speculate. We'll get the facts soon enough. As El Cap says, the main thing is we're safe. And the tinnitus, ringing in the ears, should be temporary and diminish in an hour or so."

I embraced the luxury of breathing air, being alive. Vibrations from the engines soothed me like a warm hand stroking my hair. In professor mode, he answered sporadic questions about the possible eruption then conversed more privately with the young love birds. I closed my eyes and revisited the cave art and all the day's events implied.

The afternoon sea breeze kicked in. Waves spiked a little and the humidity skyrocketed. My dream came true. Then, the world turned upside down.

El Cap radioed Isabelle to report his passengers and her vessel were safe. She asked if he noticed any floating fish since there was a small fish kill at the harbor. "No, none." he said and asked, "Why? What did you hear?"

"Earthquake."

He eased the sleek vessel up the canal and to the dock where Isabelle and half the islanders lined up. She jumped up and down, waving a linen dinner napkin over her head. Fear creased her face.

I hopped from my shaded perch to give Lonnie ample space to tie *Sweet Pea* to the dock. Blue scurried to the bow and hitched the forward line across pilings. While I gathered my near-empty gear bag, he walked toward his daughter. When he reached her, they had a quiet conversation. She nodded, eyes threatening a squall.

"There, there, baby gull," her father said. He hugged and consoled her. "We'll figure this out and rise to the top. Don't we always?"

Wow. I heard him. Overheard him. Maybe my eardrums were on the mend.

Lonnie's body language changed and her face grimaced. She spat the words, "I hate her." Damn, she can't mean me, I thought.

Before we could disembark, Isabelle peppered her brother with questions. He raised a hand to his ear and shrugged. Between the engines rumble, scores of people talking and earlier assault on his ears, it was impossible to understand her. She got the point.

The second his feet hit land, Isabelle rushed for him. "So

we'll be gettin' aftershocks and tsunamis, brother?" She twiddled the fabric of her faded apron.

"No tidal waves for Bimini," Blue said loud enough for eavesdroppers around them to hear. A happy shout erupted from the little crowd. He draped a protective arm around his sister then glanced over his shoulder toward *Sweet Pea*. Lonnie was on the floating dock where she uncoiled a fresh water hose.

"Let me go upstairs to my computer and make a few inquiries." He delivered the request in a heavier than usual accent with an upper class clip.

Blue bent down to his anxious sister and planted a tiny kiss atop her silver hair. He turned to me. "When this business is sorted out, I'd like you to come to my flat."

I leaned in toward him, my eyebrows raised.

He stammered a little. "To, to continue our conversation about what we saw. And look over some photos."

I nodded. "Sure."

He walked toward the building. I didn't want to move, just wanted three seconds to close my eyes and breathe. Isabelle waited for me.

"Are you okay?" she asked.

I nodded, shot the middle finger at my ears, shrugged, and said with a half-smile, "Ears are in shock. And so is the rest of me. And yes, I saw it."

Tears ran down her cheeks. "It wasn't supposed to happen like this."

-5-

Day Two

Blue slowed his long-legged pace. Isabelle and I caught up with him.

"I hope you're better now?" He questioned.

I nodded a white lie.

"I'd best carry on." He let out a soft sigh and resumed his hurried gait.

Isabelle and I walked arm-in-arm toward her dining hall where delicious supper aromas hitched a ride on the stiff after-noon breeze.

"Coconut telegraph say the earthquake was a blast," Isabelle said, referring to islanders name for fast moving gossip.

Part gossip, part truth, I usually ignored telegraph gos-sip. But not today. Today it was dead on the money. My eyes opened wide and so did my mouth. "And what do you say?"

"Not an earthquake," she said and let go of my arm. "Talk later. Gotta go in and help. Folks wanna eat and have company when we get a bit o' trouble." She hurried through the kitchen's worn out screen door.

Feeling alone and abandoned, I turned to people-watching. Locals with locals, tourists with other visitors. I recognized a few from our morning dive who were chatting, probably about the experience from a subsea perspective. The Jersey dive club guys smiled and said hello as they walked past me and climbed up to their rooms. I meandered down to the restaurant.

My bottom had barely touched the bar stool when Percy started my hydration and libation therapy. He set me up first with a glass of water and a then an ice-cold Kalik Gold.

"You drink water first," he said and wagged a forefinger. I saluted him and downed the water. I was parched. He smiled and said, "What you think of the blast?"

I pointed to my ears. "Think I'll be wearing hearing aids the next time we see each other. You and Isabelle both say blast."

"Huh. That no quake. Your ears, everybody ears what was underwater, they all have the ringing, yes?" I nodded. "No quake does that." He wrinkled his forehead, buried his chin in his muscular neck and peered over his glasses. Someone from across the bar hailed him so he left me to focus on the other needy patron. Isabelle scooted behind the bar, basket in hand. She winked at me as she confiscated lemons and a bottle of Angostura bitters. A patron hollered out for a beer so she set the basket down and pulled him a mug of heady brew.

I sipped my cold drink and surveyed the scene. Usual gathering. I gave a half-hearted wave to Jane, across the room playing ring the hook with a good-looking local. Cougar, I thought. Beside me sat an elderly local couple. I eavesdropped best I could with virtual cotton in my ears. I leaned in and managed to keep from cupping a hand behind my ear.

"Not a quake. Can't be. It's an explosion from the marina job," the man said in his staccato voice. He poked air with a crooked forefinger, emphasizing each word.

"So you keep saying. How you know?" the woman replied

in an exasperated tone. She sipped from a small, glass Coke bottle. I gulped beer.

"I been on dis island all my eighty years. Foreign folk come here before and rig a plan. Dynamite. One man say it's fine to blast away coral. Bimini needs rich folks' boats to dock here a while, to spend money, yes."

She was slow to reply.

First Isabelle, then Percy, now this gentleman. An illegal blast, not a quake. I was angry and my hands trembled with the knowledge. My moment of triumph was trumped and trampled. Even worse, island life was threatened and I had come uncomfortably close to being another casualty of greed. I let my chin drop to my chest and closed my eyes.

As the woman spoke, her words were softer. I strained to hear.

"True. I wanted to forget how the foreign ones came here, fished with devil sticks, blew de reef and fish flew to the sky. He does more than thief, he does murder."

He reached over and dabbed her tears with a cocktail napkin.

Blue sauntered in, obviously fresh from the shower. He sported a billowy ivory-hued linen shirt and matching trousers. He ducked behind the bamboo and plywood bar, pecked a kiss on Isabelle's high cheekbone and said something. She nodded then looked straight at me as she bee-lined it back to the kitchen. Greeting Percy, he proceeded to fix himself a drink.

"Hello Sirena," he said and came around to the stool next to mine.

I swiveled to face him. "So. What's the latest on our quake, Doc?"

His surreal eyes locked with mine before he announced in a big, king-of-the-class voice, "Folks. Care for some good news?" He paused a couple of beats. When the racket was down to a low buzz, he announced, "No evidence of a tremor." A few shouted their happiness to a scattering of applause. I'm sure the local authorities will get to the actual cause in the next day or so."

Someone in the room boomed, "Hear, hear!" Most of us raised our drinking vessels toward Blue. Close to fifty patrons cheered the news and the good news messenger. The lively patrons socialized over tables filled with plates of steaming pigeon peas and rice. Bottles and glasses cluttered table tops, signs of a busy and prosperous afternoon.

The elderly gentleman I had eavesdropped on earlier rose up and threw a laser stare at Blue who broke the fixed stare. The gentleman slowly scooted back his companion's chair and offered his hand. They shuffled to the glass door and exited.

Blue shook off the stink eye attack, leaned in and whispered, "El Cap went out to fetch your gear."

Our incident, the beer and lack of nourishment left me punchy. "That's it? No quake, ask the real questions tomorrow. All these people turning blind eyes? What's really going on, what're you scared of?" I anxiously swiveled the squeaky seat and slammed my hands on the bar.

He slid on to the stool, folded his arms and shook his head. "I'm not afraid. I'm furious. At whom? Choose from a cast of characters starting here and running clean over to Nassau. What rings true is, one way or another, anything done in a warped notion of progress is accepted, embraced. The methods of development sometimes employs dirty deeds with dire consequences. But the deeds are near impossible to prove. A host of Biminites are so desperate for jobs, they ignore environmental repercussions. Big money talks. Little Bimini stutters."

I bit the inside of my bottom lip and concentrated on one phrase, 'impossible to prove' as I started to hatch a plan.

"What if we can prove there was a blast? Then the Nassau authorities would stop the dredging. We have to work fast. If we get a storm, sand and debris might cover up their dirty tracks."

"Nassau authorities? They bought into this whole Bimini commerce strategy. And yes, even the storm would work in their favor," he said in a low growl.

"Who'd do something like this? And why did you lie to the masses?"

Clenched teeth and jaw muscles visibly jumped as he stared ahead for long seconds. I'd struck a nerve.

"I have no proof, so it wasn't a lie." He spat out the words.

"Well, I say we get to the bottom of it." I waved at Percy. "When you get a chance, busy man." I waved a cocktail napkin over my head. He rolled his eyes, dropped his shoulders and slowly marched toward me. "You in a hurry?"

"No, just hangry," I ordered a BLT and beer.

"Look, I'm exhausted. I'm gonna eat a late lunch, now, then I'll head up for a tub soak before I nap. Around tenish I'll be better and it will be supper time. What say I order dinner for two and have it sent to my room?"

He reacted as if someone threw ice water on him, a non-verbal gasp. "I'm surprised you let this derail your focus. Your five-year quest fruited, your hunch, your gut was proven. But instead of continuing on the path, you discard your catch and latch onto another issue. Curious."

"Look. If I, we, somebody doesn't do something about illegal blasting, this whole island will be a disaster zone. Reefs covered with sand, the cavern collapsed and no more access to the art. Don't forget the event today could've killed me, you, innocent masses." I stopped a half minute to breathe.

On the exhale I blew out the words, "I absolutely have to recharge mentally and physically. And, and process. Lots of processing." I sipped my drink and threw him a sideways glance. His ice water face changed to unreadable. I kept yapping.

"Oh, and in case you haven't noticed, I got all this going for me." I stood and did a quick Vanna White with my hands, pointed to my tangled hair, my salt infused sweat shirt and thrust out my sunblock-greased face.

As I stood to leave, he found his voice. "Yes, indeed."

I started for the door then stopped and asked Percy to have the BLT sent to my room. Over my shoulder I said, "You may want to slip on a pair of swim trunks under those fancy Italian britches. See ya upstairs, say ten o'clock?"

He watched as I inched my way toward the door.

● ● ●

Right before midnight, Blue and I motored across the channel from South Bimini to North Bimini Isle. Whitecaps slapped the thin wooden hull on the borrowed skiff and a blanket of clouds blocked all but a few bright stars. Our hope to cross in silence was dashed, the ancient outboard sounded like marbles swirling in a blender. I pulled out a flashlight from my big straw bag to shed some light on the shoreline and the dock. He cut the loud engine and let the homemade skiff drift toward the floating dock. We tied-up the rickety tub and hoofed the short walk to tiny Alice Town. Most of the island's action takes place near there, home of the Lucky 13 Casino and Marina.

North Bimini is a mere 700-feet wide, seven miles long with Alice Town, the designated party town. Two and three-story buildings peek between small, wooden huts painted proud Bahama blue, conch pink, sunshine yellow and other bright hues. Many businesses are established in the front with the owners residing on the second floors or the back of the buildings. Skinny lanes snake between the buildings. In the daytime and especially on the weekends, the town has the feel of a straw marketplace with people bustling in and out of the island-style huts. Hints of savory dishes float on the night air.

"It's a strong possibility we can't access the harbor in front of the casino."

"We can scope it out and come back tomorrow," I said with more confidence than I felt. I shifted the heavy handbag from one shoulder and hiked it up on the other.

Pinching my nose and coughing I said, "Good Lord, what a stench."

He grinned and motioned me to follow him behind Jay's Diner. The kitchen door opened to the canal side. Fifty feet from the back door was a pile of conch shells. Six feet wide and four feet tall, it was a conch shell cemetery.

"Remind me to come back here and pilfer a few of these beauties. They'd make swell souvenirs. And the price is right."

He laughed a deep musical ha ha ha. "You smart in a bad way."

Lucky 13 was packed with a cosmic collection of people and hummed with action as folks tugged at ugly machines spewing awful tunes. All my senses were assaulted in the plastic palace. We took turns on a one-armed bandit and then paused at the roulette table, feigning interest.

He motioned his head toward the back door and we slipped outside to the terrace and designated smoking area. A few stood around puffing on their tobacco of choice while others cozied up in ultra-cushy love seats and chairs. Giant fans whirred and toyed with the air and smoke.

Away from the softly lit terrace and closer to the shoreline, I realized the significance of the fans. They helped to stifle the stench. I breathed through my mouth. "What a sacrilege the way the fish and crabs were murdered. And to jump in this carnage." I shivered and he shushed me.

Tacky yellow tape and orange cones blocked access to the little beach and the half built slips and docks. We ducked under the no-no tape, went down three small steps, crossed the squishy, ripped-up lawn and onto the shoreline.

Soft lights from a trio of well-spaced pole lamps shimmered on the wet sand littered with death; coral, fish and open mussel shells. The stiff wind ensured my nostrils processed each and every odor.

Blue looked touristy with a camera strapped around his neck. Tight swim trunks made a visible underwear line beneath his trousers. I lay a towel on the sand and then dumped the contents of my straw bag on it. A couple of masks and an underwater light tumbled out. We dropped our outer garments in the bag, donned masks and eased into the dirty water. I held the light, he the camera. We picked our way through bloated fish on the surface and swam in front of a boat slip. I gagged and almost lost my BLT. We kicked out about six yards toward a red buoy. Straight down from the buoy was the excavation site. We dived down and shined the light across a dirty crater. I gave the okay signal in the light beam and with pinky and thumb waved the hang loose sign. Back on the surface, we took deep, long breaths and dived down to document the mayhem.

He squeezed off a couple shots of the crater filled with uprooted coral and other dark debris. Surfacing again for air, we heard loud voices then spotted silhouettes. On the beach side of the yellow no-no tape a trio of men waved their arms and shouted.

"Get out of the water and up here. Now," the biggest one yelled. His English was tinted with an East European accent. One of his partners beamed us with a blinding light.

We kicked over to a shallow spot and stood in chest deep water. He passed me the camera and I immediately sank down and swam underwater to a piling and then turned on the light. I looked for a place to stash the camera and light. For the first time ever, I was happy to see a discarded golf cart battery. Both contraband tied to the blessed trash, I surfaced, gulped air and treaded water toward Blue, who was in a glaring spotlight. He raised one hand and used the other to shade his eyes from the blinding light. He said in his best Bahamian lilt, "But of course, gov'nah."

"Where's the other one?" The big guy grunted.

"Oh. This is a bit sticky. You see, she had to go under. To get her suit."

The three looked at each other, one propped his hand on a hip pistol.

"You do recall the *Pina Colada* song?" Blue took slow deliberate steps toward the men.

I popped up behind Blue.

"Oops." I pretended to shrug on a bikini top and winked at the burley dude and his bookend kooks.

We exited the water together and headed for our towel. The three stooges watched us dry off and pull on street clothes over our wet swim suits.

"May we buy you gentlemen a round? For your troubles, hum?" Blue said.

The big guy said, "Get out. Don't come back."

"But of course. Good evening, gov'nah."

I could feel their eyes on my wet shape as we speed walked away. I heard a phone chime the *Bad to the Bone* tune.

"Not so fast." We froze then turned, slo-mo. The big guy had a phone to his ear. He pointed toward my handbag.

One of the little kooks caught up with us. He grabbed then pawed through my bag. The goon rooting through my purse and the other small man looked like twins.

"Hey, gimme back my bag, you perv," I hollered and struggled to gain control of the bag. He rifled through and tossed it back. The other one drew his hip pistol and body-blocked Blue. Hands raised, he slowly stepped away from the gunman and carefully turned to face the big guy with the phone. "Tell him to put that thing away."

The big guy made a quick head motion as he spoke in the

phone, "Yes, boss lady." He stared until the gunman reholstered the pistol. I noticed he kept a hand on the grip.

He let out a sigh and whispered to me, "None other than the Ick Brothers, Frick and Frack. Plus their steroid-popping leader, Zander."

We could hear a woman screaming over the phone. She certainly had some pipes on her.

"Get out of here and don't come back," Zander growled.

Blue took my arm and we retreated. Over his shoulder he said, "Direct orders from Dragon Lady, I presume."

Fleet footed, we hightailed to where we left the sputtering boat, our freedom float. Nothing but sand greeted us. Our borrowed boat was gone. We retreated to the water taxi.

None other than Zander waited on the dock of the water ferry. So cliché, I fully expected him to whip out a gleaming knife blade to pick his nails or teeth. When the ferry docked at South Bimini, a handful of harried passengers hopped off and veered toward their destinations. Two men we recognized as Hideaway guests. We rode over with Zander and a couple others. When we disembarked and headed toward the Hideaway, Zander shadowed us like a bad guy in a gum shoe movie. He stuck around outside, jockeyed for a comfortable chair and pulled it close to the back door. He made himself at home.

"Go on up and shower the filth off," Blue said. We peered out the window at Zander. "I need to let Isabelle in on the situation."

Isabelle wasted no time in turning her wrath on the interloper. She marched out the back door and leered. "Get off my property," she said through clenched teeth.

"Oh, finally some service around here. I'll have a water," Zander said. He sucked his front teeth and added, "A wedge of lime, lots of ice."

She kept her angry eyes on him, her fury palpable. "Huh, I'll give you service, right out of here with a royal escort."

She phoned the police to report a trespasser. Unhappy with their reply, she slammed the phone receiver down onto the old fashioned cradle.

"Unless he broke the law, he got every right to enjoy the public establishment, the sergeant say."

Zander's hot glare pierced the glass door.

"He harder to shake than a hungry shark in a bait ball," Isabelle said with a shake of her head.

~ 6 ~

Day Three

B right and early Isabelle phoned Lonnie and asked if she could conduct her morning swim in the harbor instead of the Lucky 13 pool. She told her why she needed to go there and where to find the camera.

Lonnie said, "Anything to help. I'm so mad. And ashamed."

"Baby gull, I'm sorry to pull you into this mess but you our only chance."

"It's all right," she sniffed and then hung up.

Zander's assignment was to watch over Lonnie during her morning training. He wasn't pleased to stand watch by the harbor. He preferred the pool where he could sit under an umbrella and watch half-naked women.

She lumbered out of the harbor, camera in hand. Zander was right beside her. He lunged for the camera. She hid it behind her back and he moved to snatch it from her. She turned and ran. Clearly she had an advantage, young swim champion versus burly goon in a suit.

When he caught up with her, he snagged the camera.

"What's your problem? I found it bobbing along. It's mine."

He eyed the small, yellow undersea camera with a built-in flash. "You swim in a harbor with stinking fish, not the clean pool. Then you come up with a camera."

He dialed a number and handed the phone to Lonnie. She held the phone to her ear and chewed on a fingernail.

"I hate you!" she screamed. Tears streamed down her up-turned face. She drew back and pitched the phone in the harbor.

"You shouldn't a done that," he said. "Now your mother's real mad. You and me, we both in trouble."

Lonnie hissed, "Not mother, you mean Dragon Lady."

From an inside jacket pocket, he pulled out a ringing phone and then a handkerchief. He mopped his brow and watched his young charge stomp off.

"Yes, boss lady." He listened intently as his eyes followed his charge.

In a loud voice, he shouted to the retreating teen, "She says you behave. Wants to know if you stupid enough to tell folks things they shouldn't know?"

Lonnie froze just before she jumped on her bicycle. She was hyperaware of organizations, all kinds of people who had crossed her tyrant mother and was uncomfortably aware of the consequences. Her face grew hard from the words. She pivoted to face the man. "You tell Mother Mary Grace she's set a record low, even for a barracuda such as herself."

● ● ●

I was getting great sleep when a loud voice woke me up. Two mornings in a row a falsetto voice squawked something about bitches.

Tamping down my temper, I said real loud, "Sirena, get a grip and move your ass." Free from the bedcovers, I crouched on the floor, real low. I duck walked to the disturbing noise. With stealth I moved a bunch of sheers aside so I could look out the window. When I popped up for a sneak peek I saw the noise maker. Perched on the window box was a big bird. A macaw maybe. Never could remember bird species. I'd rather swim with a shark than be in the same room with fowl. A big, red bird with a nice-size beak was cursing outside my window. I stood up and faced the bird, all brave since we had glass between us. "Who you callin' bitch? Bitch."

Bird took a look at me, flapped its gorgeous wings a bit then settled down. It stared, feathers puffed out. Rain began to dot his feathers as it re-perched on the window box.

My knuckles found the pane and knocked a loud cadence. Big bird took flight.

Later on this may hit me as funny. Wide awake, I dressed and then jaunted down to find a little coffee to go along with my worries.

"Morning, glory," Isabelle said. She tapped the chair next to her.

I sat and then locked eyes with her table mate. "Sleep well?" Blue asked.

Looking from him to his sister I answered, "Okay, except for one crazy bird."

They shot curious glances. Before they could inquire about the damn bird, Jane showed up and interrupted. "Morning. Who all's diving today?"

The three of us looked at each other as if to say, "Is she for real?"

Jane selected a large mug from the sideboard and helped herself to coffee and our table. Coffee spilled from the mug in one hand while she used the other to drag a chair over and cozy up to Blue.

"Geeze, you guys look miserable, even for a rainy Monday. What's up?" She elbowed Blue playfully.

Isabelle quipped, "Oh we're just under a hurricane watch and recovering from a bit of illegal blasting." She'd hear it sooner or later so Isabelle filled her in on our theory. Left out was the part about foiled night photography and Zander's overt antics.

"That sucks. Rumor I heard was island kids did a little midnight dynamite fishing."

First she wants to dive in a storm and now she thinks locals destroy their own life's blood. I threw her a go to hell look and muttered, "Unbelievable."

"Hey what's that for?" Jane said, wearing a prickly look.

Blue said, "I'm sure she's just sleep deprived and worried."

"Whatever. Is the dive on or not?" Jane asked.

He turned down a thumb and shook his head. "No go. We don't take divers out when the seas are four feet and we're under a watch." He gave an apologetic shrug and then took a sip of his coffee.

Jane screwed up her face and said, "Oh, yeah, the storm." She pulled finger air quotes around her words.

She got up and walked to Percy, leaned over the bar and announced, "Well, "I'm famished. Percy will you take my order, please?"

Percy jotted down her requests and rang a bell to alert the kitchen of the order. He then busied himself on the other side of the bar.

"Are you afraid of a little wind and waves?" Jane said in Percy's direction.

She didn't get a rise out of him. Just a slight shake of his head.

Too early for this much bullshit, I thought and scooted out of my chair. Blue held my arm and said, "Before you go, there's something I'd like you to see. Intel, as you are fond of saying."

I stared at his hand. He quickly released it, to my disappointment.

"What kind of intel?" Right after the words hit the airways I knew.

His face became a mask. "Meet me at my flat. I'll ask Percy to send us up a tray. Come on." He stood and then offered a hand. I took it and glanced over to gloat toward Jane's jealous scowl.

● ● ●

Lonnie slid her swim goggles down around her neck, wrapped a towel about her waist and hopped on her fat tire bike. She pedaled home lightning fast, swerving when an occasional gust would blow her off course. Rain alternated between a light mist and a steady pour.

Her wrist watch read seven fifty. A glance over her shoulder revealed her mother's spy had not tailed her. She hoped Mary Grace would be at her marina office, not at home. Lonnie imagined her greedy mother savoring an almond latte and smirking over the hijacked camera. But the teen also had a reason to gloat. She coasted over to the roadside and stopped. She wiggled the face of her watch and then slid a finger behind it. Still there. A large smile claimed her face. She finally got one over on her devious mother.

Her smile didn't linger as she hopped back on and pedaled toward home. Her headful of wet locks bobbed as she shook her head in disgust. How her control freak mother managed to have eyes and ears all over the island attested to her paranoia. And power.

Punching codes harder than necessary, she opened the street door and then repeated the ritual at the front door. Inside, she could hear Rosie Rockefeller, but couldn't see him. In the front laundry room she dropped the wet towel and snagged a dry one.

"HiLo, HiLo. Lonnie, Lonnie. HiLo."

He had been a part of the family nearly twice as long as her own fifteen years. She studied the twelve-foot ceilings in search of the wayward bird and parroted the bird's high-pitched voice.

"HiLo yourself, me Rosie buoy. Where you hiding?"

She tracked down the muffled shrieks and climbed up to the second floor. Through a window on the far side the voluminous office, she saw him perched on the outside ledge, cursing a blue streak. He cocked his head to the side, eyed her and said, "Help. Help."

"Knock it off. Be happy I'm home early, you little Houdini. Serves you right getting stuck in the rain."

She raised the window and one very wet bird hopped inside. Lonnie draped her towel around him and picked up the wild child. She spread the towel on the floor and he rolled to his back like a babe in a blanket. He nearly purred as she rubbed him.

"You spoiled devil."

Once he was drier, Lonnie took him downstairs and sat the wayward bird on a tall perch next to a six-foot tall ebonized cage. She pointed to the outside latches.

"Rosie let himself out, now let yourself in."

He examined the latches with care turning his head from side to side to give them a once over with each eye. He flew to the big cage and with his powerful talons grabbed on beside the latches. Using his beak he twisted each open. Talons still gripping the cage bars, he used his powerful lift feathers and caused the door to open. He squawked, jumped on the swinging door and took a joy ride.

When the door slowed down, he flew inside the elaborate cage. Lonnie closed and locked the door and then added a combination lock.

"Good buoy!" She reached to a side table, opened a jar of nuts and waved it around. "Come to here."

"Bitch, bitch, bitch," he said.

"Silly cuss box, you aren't the only caged one. Too bad I can't fly." She tossed a few nuts in his feed tray and covered the cage with a special blanket to keep drafts away and to keep him quiet. She ambled down the long hallway. So long, in fact, her friends dubbed it the bowling alley. She adjusted the air conditioner temp from 75 to 80 degrees, to make sure the tropical brat didn't catch cold. She headed to her own dreaded cage, her bedroom. Once inside, she reached for the landline. Before she scrubbed all the lagoon filth from her body she had to make one call.

"Auntie, tis me." She burst into tears.

● ● ●

Percy poured Isabelle a cup of hot tea as she disconnected from the landline at the bar.

"I made her miss training day. The poor child's anticipating the full wrath of Mommy Dearest. Plus Mary Grace's goon got Blue's camera. He took it away from Lonnie." She rested her head in her hands.

Percy replied, "And she'd go for the camera again. It's the right thing. Lonnie nuttin' like her Mamma, thank the Lord." He finished drying a glass and slid it overhead.

On the way out of the dining hall, Blue's mobile rang. Isabelle watched him and strained to eavesdrop on his end of the conversation. From his contorted face, she sensed it wasn't good.

"Oh no, what is it?" she begged as he disconnected.

"Mary Grace and her shark of a solicitor are circling, again. Same old game using Lonnie as bait."

- 7 -

Day Three

B lue's third floor flat was four times the size of my meager quarters, I thought as he let me in. He gestured toward a cozy living room and said, "Please, make yourself at home."

A denim-covered sofa looked appealing so I sat. In front of me was a high coffee table set with breakfast trays. I was as hungry for biscuits and gravy as I was for Atlantis knowledge.

He returned with a thick album stuck under an arm and sat close to me. He balanced the closed book half on my leg and half on his. Something in my head buzzed and my stomach tightened. I watched him fork a piece of biscuit swimming in gravy.

He covered his full mouth. "You must be starved. Go ahead."

Suddenly the thought of food made me nauseous. "Thank you," I whispered.

Sanity and five years of my life rested between us. I reached to open the cover. He spread his hand over the album and with the other he turned my head so I had to look at him. Close-up. My heart beat like drums in a Junkanoo parade.

He took a long breath. "Biminites, no one on earth will have control over the mayhem this discovery will generate. We cannot tell a soul. Not a soul. Imagine the revolution, the angst among historians, religious zealots. The opportunist looters..." his voice trailed.

I nodded. My stomach wrenched tighter and my throat constricted. With a shaky hand, I brushed his hand from the photo album and carefully cracked open the cover.

My eyes drank in a well-lit, panoramic photograph. His voice was about a half octave above the swishing in my ears.

"...murals tell a story. Difficult at first to discern since some of the pigments are a ghostly fade."

I saw a ceiling blanketed with bright constellations and highlighted by a pair of large, vivid spheres, planets. One was ruby red, the size of a grapefruit. The other, sapphire colored, looked large as a basketball. The ceiling art was hard to discern since our small flashlight beams weren't strong enough to illuminate it properly.

"On our next dive, we need to use stronger lights. I want to see everything."

"We shall." He pointed and said, "Between those two planets is a flying serpent, long as a yardstick."

Mouth agape, the green serpent sported an exaggerated tail. I could picture it snaking its way to the blue planet as if it were a spaceship. The swishing in my ears migrated to my gut and hit hard. An internal symphony raged inside me.

Overpowered by the images, the implications and my imagination, I felt my heart syncopate the internal symphony with bravado. I flipped the page and stared at another crystal clear shot. It was the cavern opening. My dream scene. Every single night for five years, this was alive in my mind. But I never dreamed of the secrets trapped beyond the entrance.

An eye witness to the cave art, yet my mind stumbled around these images. What came next punched me even harder so I pulled the book closer to inspect a detailed, complicated scene.

Prominent were three triangular structures. Pyramids. The middle one was finished and flanked by two in various stages of construction. Inside each of the unfinished was a white cylindrical shape. It was suspended in the center of the building and held up with scaffolding. People stood around several trough-looking objects rested beside each of the three. My heart and gut could no longer contain my emotions. Tears sprang from my internal well of clashing sounds.

Wiping my tears, I looked to him for answers.

"Energy sources. Crystal, we surmise," he explained as he pointed to people. "Drummers surround the pyramids. And these people hold giant drums while two others strike them."

I found my voice and interrupted. "Crystal energy? And people playing drums. The troughs – is this a … bloodletting ceremony?"

He shook his head and shrugged.

"We believe it's water-filled and channels the energy source to produce acoustic levitation."

We looked at each other and then I closed my eyes to quell the dizzy spell poised to consume my body and mind. He touched my hand and I floated back to him.

"Think Jericho, in reverse. You know, the Biblical account. Ram horns sounded to tumble down the city walls, a deconstruction; or opera singers who shatter glass with their voices. Here we see sound as a constructive tool."

The room was spinning so I closed my eyes again. Nausea subsided yet my whole being was heady from the art and his words.

Pyramids in Bimini, Atlantis pyramids and levitation, I hung on his words.

"What?" I managed to say. I clawed back to reality.

After he saw my eyes were open and I nodded, he continued, "Rocks, heavy materials required to create the pyramids, we believe they were acoustically levitated. It's an old theory, really. This image adds more credibility to the idea."

"You're serious."

"Indeed."

"Yet we can tell no one," I added.

"No, we cannot. Oh, it gets better. Or worse depending on perspective. Not only were acoustics fully understood and channeled into construction work but there's another theory." He looked at me. "But we'll go into the biological aspect later."

I nodded. Data, theories, snake-ships overloaded my every pore.

He slowly paged over and pointed to a trace of a scene. Faded shapes of people whose postures indicated attempts to escape a crumbling villa. The macabre fresco reminded me of another ancient tragedy, Pompeii.

"Do these murals document history or is it a forecast, a prediction?" I asked.

"Perhaps both. It's possible some of the Atlanteans got aggressive with the wireless energy and overpowered their city, their world. The ultrasonic frequencies perhaps sparked an earthquake."

"Impossible."

"No. Actually Tesla caused earthquake tremors in his laboratory. And he used a very similar theory and materials to generate and to successfully transmit wireless energy."

He gave me a couple minutes to digest his words.

"There's one more image but it's so powerful, perhaps we should save it for later."

I shook my head. After all, my dream sparked the overwhelming revelations. "Go on."

He flipped to the last page and then looked at me for long seconds. "This is what jolted me." He kissed the tip of his index finger and touched my nose with the proxy kiss.

A gumbo of emotions pulsed through my veins. My long sleeve mopped a tidal wave of tears. Blinking rapidly to refocus I breathed deeply and looked down.

Pyramids and an entire city were scrambled and torn in bits and pieces along the seabed. Above the submerged ruins, directly below the waterline floated a mermaid. Her unruly red locks fanned out, octopus-like and housed seahorses and tiny fishes. Her face was devoid of features.

Next to the faceless beauty was an ebony skinned merman with piercing blue eyes. His posture indicated he was holding sentinel over the mermaid.

"Spooky. It could totally be caricatures of…" he finished my sentence, "You and me."

I took possession of the entire album and balanced it on my lap. I gnawed a fingernail.

"Indeed. Isabelle was the first to make the connection."

I stopped biting my nail and said, "Isabelle. She told you everything about me. Crazy Sirena."

It was his turn to take deep, cleansing breaths. He shook his head. "Not crazy Sirena, never crazy. My sister and I are familiar with these kinds of visions. You see, Zantae shares her visions with Isabelle. You remember Zantae, our local visionary who claims ancestry to Atlantis people, the Mer Tribe? My sister was positive your vision had merit so she shared it with Zantae. And with me. Long story short, El Cap and I honed in on your cavern description. During spring break I was here and we dived the spot until we stumbled on the trapdoor to the art cave."

He ran a hand across his cropped hair and added, "Our inner circle is small. You, El Cap and I have first-hand knowledge. But the art historian, nor Isabelle or Zantae have seen the site."

"What do you mean Zantae's visions? What does she know about me, about all of this?"

He shook his head. "Zantae shares her visions with Isabelle, a connector." He paused for a minute before adding, "Isabelle has a gift of interpreting. Visionaries are naturally drawn to her. I can't give you logic. But I can swear it's true."

He walked to a bank of windows overlooking the canal. Rain pelted the panes.

"Simply put, I don't know how to proceed." He ambled back to the breakfast tray, picked up his coffee mug and sipped what must be cold brew. He cleared his throat.

I thumbed through the album, mesmerized and speechless.

"Impressions from the art professor are as profound as the images you hold," he said.

Wanting him to continue, I vowed to stay silent. I stopped leafing through the book and looked up.

"Clearly there are similarities to Egypt and the Yucatan pyramids. And the art." He sat beside me and flipped to the page showing the feathered serpent flying toward a blue planet.

"Both Egyptian and Mayan cultures share this concept, a vessel from what we figure is the red planet Mars to blue Earth."

Words got all locked up between my heart and my head. He pointed to the scene.

"We had the coppery gold material tested."

I examined the pyramids and the tonal levitation scene. Here and there were spatters of what appeared as pure copper painted on the pyramid top and the troughs.

"Conclusive. Orichalcum. Until recently it was deemed mythical. Treasure divers found dozens of the ingots, copper-based, aboard a three thousand year old Greek shipwreck near Sicily."

"Orichalcum is the best link we have to gain scientific credibility. Plato wrote Atlantis structures were blinding with the ore. Mayan temples are lined with the same basic compound but gold based. We have it here and can't do a damn thing about it."

– 8 –

Day Three

Jane cradled her cell phone. "Get me the underwater photog who shot my Florida treasure story. You know, what's his name?" She paused to listen. "Yeah, him and his sidekick. No talking head required. The whole island's buzzing, a docu-drama made in paradise. Could be a two-banger."

Propped up on her queen size bed, Jane snuggled under a quilt, fat pillows cushioned her back and head. The ancient air conditioner was turned so cold it coughed as condensation seeped along the windows of her three-room suite.

"Lemme spell it out for you. One. Local islanders versus foreign investor money. There's illegal blasting of the harbor bed to make deep water passage and docks for mini-cruise ships to dock along North Bimini. The ships will haul a butt load of passengers from Florida to North Bimini. Daily." She cocked her head, listening. Then replied, "Yep, ching ching." She took a long drag from a menthol cigarette, slapped at fallen ashes and smeared them in the quilt.

"Two. The storm. Never hurts to get some after shots. Before and during would be golden, if those photog types got the balls to fly in this soup." She listened then replied, "Bimini. Bahamas for God sake. What are you, a geographic moron? Call me back within the hour. Wind's really howling and no telling how long till phone service drops." She disconnected then snuffed out the cigarette in a saucer on the nightstand next to a no smoking sign.

● ● ●

Blue walked me back toward my room, hand to the small of my back. More to keep me steady than a caress. I've known this man for less than a week and we have as much history between us as the ocean is deep, I thought.

"I can't stay cooped up here for long. I'll head to my usual roost in the dining hall," I said.

"Your humor rises again." He gave a half grin.

I smiled and unlocked my door. "Humor and sarcasm have served me well." Turning to go, I added, "See you for the weather update. We'll find out if my dream comes true one minute and the next I bend over to kiss my ass goodbye."

He looked rattled by my coarse comment but chuckled. "Indeed. See you soon."

I closed the door and plopped in a chair by the tiny table, nauseated from knowledge.

● ● ●

Checking his email, Blue read a note from Mary Grace. She had shuttled Lonnie to her Jacksonville estate where she'll train with her new school's swim team and remain stateside until first holiday.

Typical for Mary Grace to sweep Lonnie from Bimini and

cut short the time he had with his daughter. She had a great excuse this time. Weather. He sighed with relief knowing his only child was safe from the impending storm. And safe from the clutches of Mother Mary Grace since she had stayed on the island.

Clicking on another email, a frown consumed his face while he read. The missive was from his University of Miami confidant, Professor Jenkins Monroe.

"I'm not sure how it happened but quite sure it's a problem," the email began. "My assistant discovered your images and my paper on the artwork. She's taken it upon herself to conduct further research. Should arrive on the island today. There's no stopping this whirlwind of trouble."

He slammed a fist on the desk. Jenkins sent the woman's name and recent snap shot. At the moment, he couldn't even give the predicament a second thought. All energy had to focus on the storms predicted path and prepping for it.

More bad news from a weather app. Hurricane Anastasia seemed to have Bimini in her crosshairs. It was now heading in from the south. Blue powered down the laptop, keeping it plugged in so the battery would stay fully charged. He surveyed his desktop and the arsenal of rechargeable batteries setting on ready in their respective chargers.

Standing, he tried to shake off Jenkins' news; the troublemaker wouldn't, couldn't get here until after the storm. First priority was to gear up and help El Cap stash *Sweet Pea* in a safe spot.

Soft rapping at the door distracted him. He headed to the doorway.

Jane pushed in and said, "Hey. Hope I'm not disturbing you."

He rested one hand on the door knob, the other busy running through his hair, watching her move to the sitting area.

"Come in, then." His sarcasm seemed lost on her. He pushed the door closed and trailed Jane. She plopped on the sofa and reached for the photo album. Blue, on the other side of the coffee table, managed to grab it first.

"How rude of me," she said with a coy grin. "Forgive me, I'm just naturally curious. Born this way and comes with the territory."

"Territory?" He stuck the album under an arm and remained standing.

"Yes. I wear a couple of hats. Casting agent is my main occupation. But I'm involved with a production company. We create documentaries. It's why I'm here."

"Do tell."

"I requested a crew to come over and document the horrible mess up in the north bay. The harbor fiasco." She tugged at her skimpy tube top.

He nearly dropped the album. "Well, they'll be lucky to secure passage. We're under a hurricane watch. Most likely it'll elevate to a warning by tomorrow."

"They'll be here," she said. "Just wanted you to be the first to know."

She eyed the food tray for two as she stood, one eyebrow raised almost to her hairline.

He extended his free arm toward the door. "After you," he said in a formal manner.

"Thank you, Doctor," she said in a flirty tone.

● ● ●

I looked around my room, knowing I'd best snap back to reality. I couldn't decide whether to go back to Blue's or downstairs. At his place, I could get a weather update from him and take another look at the photos. Stomach somewhat settled, I may try to nibble on a biscuit. Downstairs would be filled with the noisy hurricane revelers and worried weather watchers. I headed to Blue's.

My hand was poised to knock as his door flung open. I stepped back, surprised. Double surprised to see Miss Cougar exiting. Blue stood, mouth agape, album tucked under an arm.

"What a surprise," Jane purred. Clearly this heifer enjoyed the look on my face.

"Back so soon. Come in, please. Jane was just leaving."

My eyes about burned a hole in the album.

Jane's expression changed. "Don't let me interrupt. Toodles." She patted the album and then gave a three finger wave over her bare shoulder.

He stayed in the doorway and flung the door wide open.

I pointed to the album. "Have you lost your mind?" Changing course, I sprinted toward the outside stairs, preferring the pelting rain over meeting up with Jane's mocking eyes. She thumped the damn album, a sign of intimacy, I decided.

"Well, no." he answered to my fast-moving backside.

-9-

Day Three

Running on impulse and insult, I decided against going to my room and detoured. Crossing the empty back lot to the dive gear locker, I paused to catch my breath then flung open the heavy wood door and groped the concrete wall for a light switch. Light flickered and streamed across the room and its organized contents. Under racks of hanging gear was my equipment bag on the cement floor.

Unzipping the bag, I pulled out and donned the BC. Everything else except my weight pouches was in the bag. It was tough but I deliberately stomped up the outside stairs. Half-way up, I remembered my camera and slapped at the right BC pocket. It was there and reminded me of Blue. Already out of breath, the thought of him sent me back into a crazed, immature frenzy.

He swore me to secrecy yet when Cougar shows up, the bastard shares the album with her. Has to be. Otherwise why would she bother to thump the album? Her attitude insinuated, 'I know what's inside.' Hyperventilation was sure to creep up on me if I didn't stop torturing myself.

Back at my room's garish door, I unlocked it, walked in, flipped on the light and froze. Clothes, once tidy and folded in a tall chest of drawers were scattered all over the room.

My backpack was wide open, contents spilled on the floor. Thrusting my hand beneath the pillow, the cell was where I left it. Punching in TaxiMon digits, the 'No Service message' appeared and the battery was almost dead. This is sick and I am scared.

Punished for seeking the truth in Atlantis and exposing so called dredging. Stalked by goons and now ransacked by God knows who. Blue falls for Hollywood Jane's antics. Well, he and Isabelle might be accustomed to Third World politics and palm-greasing, but it's way beyond my comfort zone. Besides I got what I came for, didn't I?

I shucked out of my saturated clothes, toweled off the rain, brushed away as much sand as possible then changed into jeans and put on sneakers. Gotta lighten my load. Wet clothes went straight to the tub along with toiletries. Just essentials were loaded in the pack and my dive gear was stashed in the closet, I fled the room and this nightmare.

Behind the bar, Percy was crazy busy. Positioning my pack on a bar stool, I then walked to the kitchen and peeked in. No Isabelle. I backed out and surveyed the bar and dining crowd. All the makings of a hurricane party, even Cougar lady's boy toy was in the mix. With dive boats relegated to their docks or hurricane holes, construction at a halt and tourist-oriented businesses shuttered, a great majority of locals gathered here, Bimini's best watering hole. Jukebox music joined the light roar of conversation with a heavy dose of alcohol-induced posturing.

I moseyed over to my pack and pure chaos to vie for Percy's attention.

"Hey Percy," I hailed, waved and then waited for him to take some drink orders. Percy never wrote down a single order. No matter how complicated, it was all in his head.

"Yes ma'am. He peeked at my backpack. "Leaving so soon?"

I shrugged. "Got to." Can I used the bar phone? Mine's dead."

From under the bar he produced an ancient black rotary desk phone. "No long distance."

"Sure." I dialed the TaxiMon number from memory and left a message.

Fifteen minutes later a car pulled under the overhang and blew the horn. Repeatedly.

Percy said, "Must be your cab."

"Yeah."

I shouldered my pack and handed Percy a folded cocktail napkin and my room key.

"Please give this to Isabelle." He nodded as he dropped it in the front pocket of his flowery shirt. I leaned over and kissed his cheek then palmed my camera to him. His eyes squinted, pleaded a silent 'what the hell'. I put a finger to my pursed lips, "Shhh." He pocketed the tiny camera. "I'll be back," I whispered and added, "gear's in my room".

The cab driver didn't bother getting out of the front seat. He popped the trunk. I kept my stuff with me, pushed the trunk shut and then slid in the back seat.

A couple of minutes down the road he looked at me in the rear view and said, "Another customer. Be right back." This driver must be new, but hard to tell since his hipster framed glasses were dark tinted.

He parked in a horseshoe drive in front of a nice house in a locals-only kind of neighborhood. The driver pulled down his hat, turned up his raincoat collar and then marched up the steps to a typical Bimini beach house. The front porch was painted haint blue. Superstition says haints, or ghosts, can't cross water so front porches and doors often are painted a pale sea blue to thwart visits.

Maybe I should sleep in a haint blue gown.

Conch shells were displayed on each of the half dozen or so steps leading to the covered front porch. The shell openings were face down to keep ghosts from entering them, more island lore.

I tried to remember where I stashed the phone charger. When I got to the airport I'd find it and put it on charge in one of the outlets. By the time I hopped on my plane, it should be at least fifty percent. I watched two men in black raincoats hustle out the front door, the driver right behind them. Men, soaking wet white guys, slid in on each side of me.

● ● ●

Day Four

My next memory is of me slumped over, sitting on a tiny loveseat. My neck was sore and my arms felt like a swarm of bees stung them. I peeked through half-open eyes and saw a small room, no windows. All alone. I got to my feet and dizziness claimed my equilibrium. I plopped back on the sofa. My arms were numb and vision blurred. Bastards drugged me. Why? Damn, I had to get up and walk this off. Slow and deliberate, I stood and stayed vertical. I ambled to the only door.

I frisked myself. No phone. I looked around, no pack and nothing to beat open the wood door. Or was it metal? I fist banged the thick door.

"Hey, let me outta here."

The doorknob turned and the driver walked in, quickly shutting the door behind him.

I tried to keep recognition from showing on my face. He's the same ass who messed with Blue and me at the harbor, Zander.

"You kidnapped me. Let me go and I'll drop all the charges."

He laughed and let himself back out.

"Hey, goon, I'm not done with you. Get back in here." My head ached worse when I yelled. I started to kick the door but realized I was barefoot. My shoes were MIA along with my pack. I was freakin' screwed.

I did have on my watch. Time was four thirty. What day?

The room was silent, couldn't hear the wind or waves. I put my ear to the door and heard what may have been faint talking or a radio, or tv, hard to tell. The knob moved again. I shifted to stand behind the open door. Goon slammed the door with his foot. His hands were occupied with a food tray.

"You gonna poison me? Again?"

"Not poison. You're alive, yes?" He put the tray on the sofa, picked up the little loaf of Bimini bread and bit a huge hunk from it.

"I'll eat it if you won't." He said between chews.

The bread smelled heavenly but I had to focus. "What are you gonna do with me?"

He shrugged. "Not sure. Yet." He grinned a sick, gold-capped smile.

I shuddered.

"Eat," he ordered. "I'm s'possed to watch."

"Bullshit. Leave me alone."

He laughed and left.

I stashed the fork in my back pocket and ate the bread. The mac and cheese melted in my mouth just like Isabelle's. Bastard had the gall to order from the Hideaway.

Isabelle. She won't miss me for hours. Blue knows I'm pissed so if he knocks on my door and I don't answer, it won't raise any concern. I'm sure Jane will be glad to distract him some more. And who the hell tossed my room? I picked up a plastic bowl of pigeon peas and rice and flung it across the room. It hit the wall and left a nasty stain. I took some bites of fish, downed the water. In a slow pace, I checked out the place. Faint outlines marked where the windows were boarded up and dry walled in. Dear Lord, it's a torture chamber.

Sometime later, Goon ass returned for the tray. He eyed the rice and peas art on the wall but didn't comment. I wanted to stab him with the pitiful plastic fork, but it'd be like spearing a Goliath grouper with a toothpick. He's thick, mentally and physically.

"I gotta use the bathroom," I said and added, "And I need my back pack."

"Hold on, Red."

He left with the tray and shortly returned bearing a bedside potty.

"Hell to the naw. And where's my pack? I need some feminine products from it. Or do you want to run to the store for me and buy some…"

"I'll be right back."

When he returned with my pack, I realized just how soft he was between the ears.

"Thanks. Now get out I need my privacy."

He hurried out. What a simpleton.

I dug through the pack and put my hands on a nail file, my phone and the charger. But no electrical outlets. Damn. I stashed the phone in my bra and didn't have time to snag and hide the charger.

When I spied the door knob turning, I hollered, "Stop, I'm in the middle of personal hygiene." The door slammed. I bought a little more alone time. I did have to pee like a racehorse and sat down and did my business. An idea struck me. I shouldered my pack.

About ten minutes later when the door slowly pushed open, I was behind the door. Stealth, I said to myself as he peeked his head around the doorway. I waited until he came fully inside the room and pulled the door behind him. Whoosh. I sloshed the pee all over his face.

"What the fuck?" he hollered and clawed at his face. I kicked him in the nuts, ran out, slammed the door, and made sure it was locked.

I wondered if the two so called passengers were his same sidekicks as on our first encounter. Damn, they'd surely be hovering around. Quietly as possible I tiptoed over the creaky wood floors. Nothing. Nobody. The only furniture I saw was a big chair in the kitchen next to a stainless refrigerator. No table.

I hauled ass out of there. Rain poured down in buckets; the

dirt road was a river of mud. Headlights appeared. I ducked behind a giant Gumbo Limbo tree, its limbs seemed to fight with the high wind. A Jeep passed. I watched red tail lights disappear around a corner before I took up a fast pace. Damn phone was eating a hole in my chest.

I hit a big pot hole and stumbled face first into the muddy water. I stopped long enough to feel my bare feet ache. I felt like a mud wrestling floozy. My phone was saturated, toast.

Fierce barking got my attention. A big pit bull stood looking down on me. I pulled myself up to the loud growl of a mean-looking dog. Slowly I pulled off my pack and put it between us.

"Nice puppy," I said.

He turned up his nose at me and ran the other way, whimpering.

I felt triumphant until a vehicle motored toward me from a side road.

"Damn." I tried to get out of the road and hide. The Jeep skidded to a halt. Frick and Frack jumped out. I took off in the opposite direction.

-10-

Day Four

The taxi pulled close to the Hideaway's front door. Driver, Abraham, positioned the rusty old Fiat's passenger side to protect it with the building's wobbly overhang. Shoulders hunched and collar upturned, he hopped into the rain and opened the back door for his passenger. She unfolded gazelle legs covered with ragged Levis. A worn UM hoodie partially covered her eyes and an oversized rucksack was slung low on her back. Cradling a fat duffle like a football, she passed it to Abraham, catching him in the gut by surprise. He stumbled as they made their way inside.

As the new arrivals blew in the front entryway, Blue dashed out the back door and sprinted to the dock. El Cap was already aboard *Sweet Pea*. They shoved off from the dock and navigated through the channel.

Inside the bustling Hideaway, Lonnie's absence was sorely missed. Nobody else had the time or inclination to answer questions and handle myriad other bothersome yet necessary tasks. Isabelle hand-scrawled a large note on the blackboard at the hostess stand: "See Isabelle in the kitchen for lodging."

Abraham's feisty fare pointed at the sign, flung back her hood, and raised a scant eyebrow. "Do you believe this?" she sniffed in a haughty tone.

He eyed her hay-colored dreadlocks, holey jeans and muddy five hundred dollar rain boots. "Yes ma'am. You and me settle up, then I go get Miss Isabelle, yes?"

She dug in her pocket and pulled out a ten. American. "Keep the change." She sashayed to a bar stool and settled in.

Abraham pocketed the bill, dropped the duffle at the arrogant woman's feet, and then muttered to himself. "Fare nine and a half." He headed for the kitchen's open double doors.

Isabelle emerged drying her hands on a frayed cotton towel. She flung it over her shoulder as Abraham pointed out the white lady with dreads. She walked over to the bar.

"Welcome to Bimini," Isabelle said.

The young woman turned in her swivel chair.

"I need a room." she muttered from the side of her mouth. Pulling amber liquid through a clear straw.

"How many people and for how long?"

"How many does it look like you're talking to?" she said, biting the straw between pearly front teeth. "One. And let's say, five nights."

Isabelle's face flushed. She looked around. Percy was in deep, animated conversation with Abraham on the other side of the crowded bar.

"Standard question, Miss, uh…"

The woman stared with no expression.

"Name?" Isabelle said with a little more force and volume than normal.

She let go of the straw. "Holly. Just Holly."

"Five nights, even with the storm brewin'?"

Holly said, "No problem. Mon." she emphasized the last word.

Isabelle turned her head slightly. Fire smoldered in her chocolate brown eyes at the obvious slur. She motioned for Holly to follow her. On the way to the hostess stand, she mumbled something about skinning a smart ass.

"How you care to pay?"

Holly plopped down a fistful of American fifties on the wooden stand. "Cash. Need a receipt."

Isabelle pulled out the strong box and spun its combination. She counted the bills and delivered change, a receipt and a key. "Enjoy your stay. You dine here, we run a tab till your last day with gratuity at twenty percent." Isabelle indicated the bar with a nod of her head. "Over there is different. No discounts, no overnight bar tabs."

Holly over-arched an eyebrow. "Locals stick you a lot?"

"Not a t'all. Mainly cocky tourists." She turned on her heels and headed toward Percy and Abraham.

● ● ●

Wind gusts were up to 45 mph. Waves lifted *Sweet Pea's* bow and slapped her down on the stormy sea. El Cap handled the twin screws with surgical precision. He plowed up the faces of the three to five foot waves and then finessed the boat down and across the backside of the waves. While the boat was hit with a slam jolt at the bottom, the captain's focus and control kept the mighty vessel from getting swamped.

Keeping Isabelle's boat at the dock was not an option. Winds would pound the vessel to the dock and destroy both. In the middle of the bay in thirty feet of water the boat could ride out the storm at best, sink at worst.

Before leaving the dock, El Cap pre-rigged lines for gale force winds. Harder to anticipate is shifting winds, especially if the eye passed over the island. At the honey hole where the boat would stay until after the storm, the daunting task would be to set anchors to allow the boat to turn with the wind.

Blue gave hand signals to El Cap when it was time to drop anchor using an electric switch. He signaled with a downturned thumb to start and a chopping motion across his throat to stop letting the line out. The bow anchor crashed through the waves and set true on the first try.

A second, smaller anchor had to be hand dropped from the stern. Blue held up a tight fist and the captain put the engine in neutral. He tossed the anchor and pulled hard on the line to set it, face set in concentrated worry. After a half dozen attempts, the anchor finally grabbed bottom and set.

Blue kept watch on the anchor to make sure it didn't start walking across the sandy bottom. El Cap prepared the heavy duty inflatable dinghy for the half-mile bronco ride to shore. Confident the anchors would hold, the men turned to the next task, easing the inflatable boat overboard.

The captain hopped in, made his way to the stern, straddled the thick wood seat and yanked the outboard's rope start. The forty horse outboard instantly roared to life.

Engine whine and exhaust filled the air, the whine competed in decibels with whistling wind and driving rain. Blue focused on moving up to the bow. He managed to sit sideways so he could scout for dangerous debris. He positioned himself so El Cap had a clean shot to navigate. The inflatable was tossed around like a toy in a washing machine.

"Wind's shifting. Again." He cupped a hand to his mouth and hollered, "Watch out, go port!"

El Cap veered a hard left, knocking Blue off the skinny bench seat.

● ● ●

Safe from the pit bull, I got out of the street and paused to catch my breath beside a house. As the cloud-shrouded sun sank, so did my heart when I saw Frick and Frack jump out of the Jeep. I didn't wait around to see which way they'd go. I hauled-ass on a saturated lane between a row of houses. One was a shack with busted out windows. I sped for the next one, a lime green one in good shape. But plywood shutters were nailed over the long front windows. I trotted around back and tried the door. Locked. I banged on it with both fists. No answer and no way to break in. I ran straight out from the back porch and then screeched to a halt as I teetered on the edge of a crumbly seawall.

The idiots with the drawn guns careened around the house, hot on my heels.

"Holy crap," I hollered and jumped for the stinging safety of the white capped bay.

–11–

Day Four

By nightfall, storm preparations on the island kicked into high gear. Isabelle and her crew labored in the kitchen where noisy ice makers protested their increased output. Ice during hurricanes was more precious than gold. Scooping ice into waiting coolers fell to the kitchen staff's children as their parents sweated over skillets of fish and cauldrons of boiling shrimp. Most islanders, and especially restaurant owners, prepared perishables and hoarded ice before a storm. When the power failed, food would be ready to heat on gas or propane stoves.

The dining hall was filled with a few guests, extended Rolle family members and Biminites itching for a good hurricane party. Certain staff members and their families would lodge at the Hideaway to ride out the storm. Percy leaned across his bar to talk to Abraham. "How many flights went out today?" He dried a glass and slid it in the overhead rack.

Abraham shrugged. "None."

"Oh. So who'll be driving Sirena back here?"

Abraham scrunched his nose, removed his newspaper boy hat and scratched his bald pate.

"Bring back from where?"

"She hired a car to the airport."

"Nobody running. Even Rasta's ole Taxi Mon van too leaky to drive. It's just me 'n the ole Fiat." He jerked his head toward the front. "Only plane in was private. Dread-lady my only fare all day."

Percy patted his front pocket then gingerly pulled out Sirena's note to Isabelle. He motioned for Abraham to get behind the bar. "Take over for a few." He tossed over the drying cloth.

Percy wrestled Isabelle away from the stove and to a newly vacated table.

"What's wrong wid you?" she said and shrugged from Percy's guiding hands. He pulled out a chair and motioned for her to sit. She shot him a glacial look and then settled into a straight back chair, face screwed up in frustration. He handed over the folded note.

• • •

Abraham's feisty fare, Holly, didn't allow her disappointment with the lousy weather and cheap motel room to compromise her mission. She'd consider it a campy experience with a lofty payoff and headed up to the shower.

For the first time in 36 hours, she undid the white bandana holding coarse looking locks away from her make-up free face. She bent over at the waist, flung her head upside down and shook volume into tired dreads before wiggling out of mud and rain-splattered jeans and into the shower.

Clean and fresh, she headed for the excitement downstairs. The jeans were the sprayed-on look and an off-the-shoulder peasant blouse accentuated her fake tan. Fierce, golden cat eyes glowed and heads turned as she slinked to the bar.

"What's your poison?" Abraham asked Holly.

She stared directly into deep, dark eyes and barked, "Dark and Stormy. Two rocks stirred in a tall glass." She indicated a good-sized glass using both hands.

Abraham paused to take in her unusual voice and unusual order. He gave the odd beauty a double take. "You the same gull I brought over?"

"What you tink, Mon?"

●　●　●

Frick and Frack peered over the seawall, careful not to stand on the crumbling concrete where rivets of muddy water streamed into the sea. The rain had let up some, but the wind still howled from the southeast.

"She'll come up for air sooner or later," Frick said.

Frack shook his head. "She's dead. Nobody can live in the ocean during a storm like this. Boss lady gonna give us a bonus."

When a tree trunk slapped the sea wall with a loud bang, the Ick brothers jumped backward. Frack fell hard on his skinny butt.

Frick extended a hand to his mirror image and yanked him up from the mud.

"Boss lady's gonna be in one of her moods if we don't do it her way," Frick said in a chiding tone.

●　●　●

I had a death grip on a piece of half-submerged plywood and felt like I was riding an express wave to Miami. Sore, cold, scared and bleeding, I bobbed to dodge tree limbs and big hunks of bamboo. I surrendered to the tremendous rip that sucked me to the open ocean. My life was a goner anyhow once the sharks got a whiff of my fear and vulnerability.

Wham. Something hit me from behind. I scrooched both legs tight to my abdomen. Another hit. Dear God, just let it kill me quickly. Wham. A frontal attack hard enough to knock me off the plywood flotation. I treaded water and came face-to-face with my attacker.

"One Eye. You out to kill me, too?"

He didn't bust a move to hurt me so I grabbed the outer rim of his shell where the least amount of barnacles grew and hung on. His powerful flippers pushed against the water. He towed my submerged torso like a human troll line. But he wasn't going toward land. My tricked out ride was taking me out to sea.

I hysterically screamed, "Whoa. One Eye, other way. Wrong way. Recalculate." I slapped the shell. He never missed a stroke.

Changing tactics, I conjured up a cooing voice and said, "Turn around, good turtle." I patted him, exuding all the adoration of a new parent.

One Eye exhaled and took a dive. Instinctively I hardened my grip and swallowed to equalize my ears. Wherever he'd take me was far better than being on the wrong end of a nine millimeter.

Headlines flashed in my mind, *Weeki Wachee Mermaid dies riding Turtle.*

I shut my eyes from the sting of saltwater and hung on to ole One Eye. Something bumped my forehead and I gasped, sucking in liquid hell.

Uncontrolled coughing caused me to inhale like a beached whale. But instead of water I breathed air in the black echo of nothingness.

One Eye made a loud nasal whine as he inhaled with great force. I was alive and shivering in total darkness.

Convulsive coughs helped expel unwanted crap from my lungs and when I automatically inhaled, my lungs filled with beautiful foul air. Once the coughing ceased, I rubbed the goose egg forming on my forehead and kept the other firmly planted on One Eye.

Total darkness was cut by a glowing green haze. Spots of phosphorescence lived in symbiosis on One Eye's mossy back so I petted his back until most of the shell radiated. Afraid to let go of the shining turtle, I held the perimeter of his shell and hand walked to where he was angled down and submerged. I crawled up on his shell.

He sunk a bit and rocked side-to-side.

"One Eye, hold still, boy. No diving allowed." My voice echoed loud and eerie.

My feet, my whole body and mind were achingly numb. Vicious cramps attacked my toes, feet and legs. I stretched out my legs to flex my feet and kicked something solid. I knew where he'd brought me. I bent back down to lay across the handsome reptile.

I opened the double clasps of my octopus bracelet and yanked it from my swollen wrist and then shoved it up the turtle's flipper.

"It's a long shot. Don't worry, it'll eventually biodegrade." I patted toward what I hoped was his head. "Hold real still, boy." I pulled off my Rasta hair tie and slid it over and around the bracelet for good measure.

My main focus was how to get out of the water before hypothermia set in. With galvanized effort I assumed a squatted position, calves threatening to explode. My shaky legs stood and the turtle inhaled with enough velocity to raise me up. Tears flowed as I pushed through the pain and extended an arm high up and found a low ledge. I managed to hoist my tired ass all the way up. My face was planted on a cold, rough surface and I rolled over to lay flat on my back.

"You did good, boy. The cave isn't such a bad sarcophagus." He replied with an exaggerated exhalation.

"I better stay here. My shell's not as hard as yours," I squeezed the words from my parched throat.

Immune to my antics, he drew in a deep breath and hissed another great exhalation. He barely splashed, just sank deeper and deeper. I watched his glow-in-the-dark shell fade to black.

Alone and cold. I wished death would come quick like it did for Sterling on that dusty Mexican road.

~12~

Day Four

Lips moving silently, Isabelle read Sirena's note, eyebrows furrowed so tight her forehead resembled an accordion. She looked away from the note, damp eyes searching Percy's.

"Gull done lost her mind. Went off half-cocked sayin' Blue a traitor, the whole island full of greedy cheaters. Said she'll come back when he ain't here."

Percy fumbled with the pocketed camera. He shook his head. "Somehow she got it all mixed-up. Abraham says he didn't carry her to the airport. So where is she and who took her off?"

Holding the missive to her heart, Isabelle was slow to reply. "Just when she found a little peace, knowing she was right, so many tings go to the devil." She stood, swayed a bit and then put her free hand on the table to steady herself. Percy stood so fast his chair crashed backward. He put a hand under her elbow and an arm around her shoulder. They slowly ambled toward the kitchen. He helped seat her directly inside the kitchen's open doorway. A few workers eyed them but kept their harried paces.

"When you 'spect Blue and El Cap to be back?" Percy asked, leaning in the doorway.

Isabelle shrugged. "Depends." Her head bobbed toward the plywood covered windows.

"Yeah, we're all at the mercy of this weather. Royal police won't go out of their way to see about a runaway tourist."

The front door opened and a loud whisk of wind and rain accompanied a cop and a woman. Holly swiveled in the tall bar stool and eyed the pair. She swirled the ice in her half-empty glass and took a sip before returning to her game of Tetris.

The uniformed cop removed his rain soaked hat and surveyed the busy room. Almost all action ceased allowing the room's occupants to actually hear a Nat King Cole tune croon from the jukebox. Abraham was still pulling bar duty for Percy. His jaw tightened. "How can we help you, Lieutenant?" he said.

"Evening, I'd like to speak to Miss Isabelle," the Lieutenant said.

"In the kitchen," he directed the cop across the room with a wave of his bar rag.

The woman with the cop dropped the hood attached to her navy blue London Fog. "Hammm," Mary Grace purred the barkeep's nickname over her shoulder as she followed the Lieutenant to the kitchen.

Abraham stiffened at the unwanted use of his nickname. He spat, "Miss Mary Grace." He spun around and let out a "har-rumph" as he focused attention on a patron. Whispers and conversations resumed in hushed tones as Mary Grace followed in the officer's wake.

Percy stiffened as the pair pushed through to the kitchen. "Lieutenant, what brings you out in this weather?"

Isabelle folded the note and looked up.

"Just need to ask a few questions."

Isabelle eyed Mary Grace. "What she's doing here?"

"Why, Auntie," Mary Grace snipped.

"Ladies, please," the Lieutenant chided and then continued. "Miss Mary Grace is here because she filed trespassing and possible vandalism charges against a guest."

Isabelle stood and leveled a laser stare at the other woman. "Who?"

"Sirena Galanopoulos Thomas."

Isabelle was pretty sure of what Mary Grace had cooked up. "Not here."

"She formally check out?" the cop asked.

"Hours ago she took the last plane."

"Storm and all," he mused.

Mary Grace screwed her painted red lips to a sultry pout. "But Auntie, our police friend says she's not on any passenger lists."

The cop gave Mary Grace a stern look. "Leave me to my job."

Mary Grace threw up her hands. "Of course, Jack, uh, Lieutenant." She cut her eyes and a devilish smile toward Isabelle.

Isabelle said, "Well, I'm no travel agent."

Percy half-grinned.

"Then you won't mind if we look around. Help me sort this out," the officer said.

"Fo what? You know you can take my word to de bank."

"Yes ma'am. And now I take a look at her room."

Isabelle shrugged and walked to the key rack. She pretended to get Sirena's room key. "I'm gone let ya in, only you. She stays downstairs."

Mary Grace threw a four finger wave. The cop looked her

way and seemed to dare her to speak. She rolled her eyes and impatiently tapped a designer rain boot.

"Jack, uh, Lieutenant, she may be hiding up in Dr. Rolle's quarters."

"Give it a break, gull," Isabelle said between clenched teeth. Room key in hand, she motioned him to follow.

The party ambiance returned to pre-cop decibel with billiards and ring-the-hook games in full swing. Conversation flowed and serious elbow bending resumed.

Jane was in a snuggly conversation with boy toy Aiden when she spied the law man. After a quick nose peck to her young muse, she snaked upstairs.

"Hey," Aiden shouted and held up his arms.

She shrugged and blew him a kiss.

"This is getting juicy," she said to herself.

Isabelle fought to contain her anger.

"Lookin' for Sirena, then?" she asked.

"Yes ma'am."

"What kind a proof you got sayin' she did wrong?"

He let out a deep sigh. "You know I can't say."

"You not spillin' any deep secret."

"Eyewitnesses say she trespassed and evidence shows she did some destruction at a construction site."

"Says who?" Isabelle asked. She jiggled the stubborn room key in the lock and then flung open the door. Standing back, she extended her arm in an after you gesture. He bent inside to feel around for the wall switch.

He didn't answer but let out a low whistle when the overhead light illuminated the room.

"This place a mess. And she left her belongings. Why?"

"Huh, my guest had a visitor. An unwanted someone broke in." Isabelle planted her hands on her aproned hips. "Maybe I oughta file a complaint wid you."

His eyes roamed to the overturned contents of the chest, looked down at the trash strewn floor and the mattress half off the bed. He massaged the rim of his plastic covered hat with both hands.

He motioned Isabelle to stay in the doorway as he strode to the open closet and peeked in. Next he headed for the bathroom and flicked on the light. He didn't waste a minute before the light was out and indicated with a head nod toward the exit door his search was over. Isabelle turned off the light and locked the door behind them.

"You gone arrest her?"

"No ma'am, just need some answers. Will you give her this when she returns? And don't say she won't. She will be back." He gestured wide.

Isabelle let out a sigh and held out a hand. She immediately scanned the official-looking document.

"This says Sirena can't leave the island till she sign a statement. Or get arrested." She looked up from the document to a grinning punk of a man. "Anything else?" Isabelle said to the cop.

"No ma'am. Just remember to deliver this to Mrs. Thomas."

He followed her downstairs. She blew a sigh and quickly crossed herself. Heavy boot falls were the only sounds between them as they made their way to the dining room's merrymakers.

Mary Grace stood and slipped on her raincoat. The lieutenant's expression of amusement was replaced with a blank face. He fidgeted with his hat. Isabelle's own anxious hands attempted to smooth her wiry hair, ends sticking out like urchin arms. She avoided Mary Grace's fembot eyes by looking down to flick imaginary crumbs from her stain-smudged clothes.

"Well?" Mary Grace asked.

The Lieutenant shook his head. "I'll brief you later." He put on his hat.

"Take care, Auntie," Mary Grace said in a fake sweet voice.

Isabelle ambled to the kitchen. She landed on her usual spot just inside the doorway and massaged her aching temples.

~ 13 ~

Day Four

C limbing up the backside of waves, the rubberized boat groaned. El Cap throttled back and held his breath when the dinghy raced down the faces of wave after pounding wave. One hand shielded his face from the pelting rain and the other gripped the outboard's tiller. So far he'd managed to keep the boat from getting swamped.

Blue hunkered down in the bow and held a flashlight to locate and illuminate the channel markers to stay in the channel. Seawater and rain accumulated quicker than the auto bilge could keep up. Hours later, the boat neared the Hideaway's dock, the water level on the floor of the boat was ankle deep.

A sudden crosswind took control of the boat as it neared dockage. When it slammed into the dock, El Cap lost his grip on the tiller and bounced off the bench. Blue landed on his backside. Mother Ocean seemed to mock El Cap's skills and calculations. But not for long.

Blue took advantage of the boats reverb and pulled up and then steadied himself. When the boat ricocheted back to the dock, he jumped out of the boat and onto the dock, bowline in hand. He looped it over the piling like a cowboy roping a calf. El Cap was ready for the next impact. He timed his leap from the boat to the dock and secured the aft line.

A couple of kitchen workers ran out to help the men get the dinghy on a trailer. They hand pulled it to the shed. After the dinghy was secured they bolted for the sheltered comfort of the Hideaway.

"Thank God you're safe," Isabelle said. She inspected each as they made their way inside. Stomping filthy mud onto the coconut fiber rug, they simultaneously slid out of rain gear. Isabelle draped towels around their shoulders.

"*Sweet Pea's* anchored out in a bay cove, our usual honey hole. Should be fine," El Cap reported, toweling his long locks.

Their helpers carried off all the saturated outerwear. Isabelle plied the drenched men with more towels and followed them to the bar where Percy resumed his duties. A carafe of hot tea was in front of the only empty seats. Next to the tea cups were shots of whiskey.

Isabelle stood over her brother and El Cap. "Finish your tea then both of you get upstairs to change. There's clothes for you both up in Blue's room." She patted each on the back. "Come back, licitly split. Mo' than one storm a brewin' tonight."

His sister walked away before he could make an inquisition.

As the men set the empty mugs on the bar, a feminine voice spoke from behind them.

"My goodness, welcome back. We were so worried about you."

He spun the chair toward the voice. Jane. She picked up the draped towel and slowly rubbed it across Blue's bare arms. "Looks like you may need a little help with your body heat."

El Cap raised an eyebrow and looked down his nose at Blue, who blushed.

"Kind of you, Jane." He yanked the towel from her grip.

She replied, "Your sister is right about another storm. So, once you've dried off, I can fill you in on the rest. Oh, how the proverbial undercurrent splits this little isle apart." She winked and sashayed back toward Aiden.

• • •

Mary Grace smiled as she slid in the passenger side of the luxurious Hummer. She patted the leather seat, content with herself for the role she played in getting a top-shelf vehicle for the police. Not the first time she was generous with the Royal Police and it won't be the last.

The Hummer's previous show-off owner turned out to be the main competitor in her bid for the coveted marina expansion contract. Under the pretense of partnering with him on the contract, she spent a few sordid nights over cocktails with the rich Dutch developer. She gathered enough info to hand over to her personal assistant who went to work uncovering possible dirty deals in a previous Bahama condo development. Naturally Mary Grace double-crossed the Dutch construction guru and he offered the Hummer as a peace offering, thinly disguised bribe, and immediately withdrew his bid. The rest is history; Mary Grace won the entire contract and racked up another proud moment.

After the officer had pain-in-the-ass Mary Grace inside the Hummer, he half slammed the passenger door, paused a beat, stuck a forefinger to the wind and let out a long "hummm".

Settled behind the wheel, he turned over the engine and turned on the conversation.

"Seems like the wind's laying down." He put the vehicle in gear then added, "Tell me, Mary Grace. Why would a vandal take incriminating photos of her own handiwork?" He pulled out of the flooded parking lot and kept his eyes on the dark, muddy road.

Mary Grace stiffened. "I thought you understood. In an attempt to frame the company, she rigged the dredging site to appear as if we employed, um, unauthorized methods. By the way, you did get the camera."

"No camera. What unauthorized methods?"

She cleared her throat. "You saw the photos."

"I saw blurry thumbnails which could be a dirty pool bottom. Statements issued by marina employees aren't exactly evidence, either."

"What matters is she trespassed, we have eye witnesses. And she vandalized; we have photos."

"Let's be clear. Yesterday afternoon there was a blast, not last night. Tell me what implicates Mrs. Thomas. And your ex-husband."

The windshield wipers beat a steady cadence. Mary Grace's face twisted at the mention of Blue and hints of suspicion. She looked down to fiddle with her neck scarf and adjust the already cinched belt. "I won't drag my child's father into this mess. Besides he's an educated Biminite without a blemish."

After a very pregnant pause, she continued. "This outsider tricked him. He's adverse to the marina project. She used her charms and his sentiment as bait."

The cop cut his eyes to Mary Grace, a powerful figure whose vengeance was legendary.

Looks like he placated her tonight. Anybody else and the outrageous request would've died on the clerk's paper-riddled desk. At the end of the day, only the proverbial little people were sore. They'd get over it.

He parked and walked Mary Grace to the front door of her south island cottage. The street door to the tiny fortress swung open before her outreached hand could touch the keypad.

"Boss Lady," said the refrigerator of a man. He held open the door. Without missing a step, she nodded in his direction and marched toward the house.

She didn't bother to invite him in. "Be safe, Jack," she called over her shoulder.

Inside, she held the dripping raincoat on the tips of her manicured fingers, tapped her foot impatiently until Refrigerator fetched it.

● ● ●

Percy pulled the brass dinner bell rope repeatedly and the room resounded with an ear piercing, off-key bing, bing. A high soprano couldn't overpower the deafening bell. Silence permeated the room and Percy turned on the NOAA radio for the latest update.

Blue and El Cap walked in as the bell sounded. They made their way through organized chaos and edged into their usual spots in time for the robo voice to report weather, "…no longer stalled on the edge of Bimini, yet the tropical storm has become the first named storm of the season, Hurricane Anastasia. The prediction is the category one storm could increase to a two before making landfall. Models indicate landfall to make the Fort Lauderdale area, but more..." the canned voice was drowned with hoots and cheers. The revelers, most well into their cups, had dodged disaster.

"Saved by the bell," Aiden hollered. The noise resumed its pre-news level.

Isabelle said, "Curfew lifted." She knew they'd party somewhere into the not-so-far away wee morning hours. May as well take advantage of the cash flow.

A palpable feeling of relief sizzled. Isabelle raised her tea-cup and cheered with the crowd.

"You have our good news. Come to the kitchen for the rest."

El Cap and Blue followed her to the kitchen.

● ● ●

Raising a heavy arm to my chapped face, I squinted at my glow-in-the-dark dive watch. It was stuck at eight twenty-two. I had no idea how long I'd been on the subaquatic slab and couldn't believe I was alive. At least I thought I was alive. Was this hell? The chilling cave and its utter darkness wrapped around my soul.

I called out in a weak, dry voice, "One Eye, come." Sloshing water answered. No turtle.

Gotta come up with a plan. I rolled and fell into the water, it was much warmer than my own skin but weighed me down. So much for a plan.

Like an anchor, I dropped to the bottom. Hands flared, fingers open wide, I slapped around for the opening and snagged the tagline Blue had planted. I jettisoned through the escape hole and into the cavernous overhang. With both my aching feet, I pushed hard against the cavern roof. The downward momentum sprung me out. My head throbbed and lungs screamed for air.

Arms thrust overhead I leveled off and dolphin kicked toward precious air. Finally on the surface I flipped on my back and breathed greedily. Waves rocked me and water poured across my face. I resorted to treading water. At the top of every wave crest, my eye scoured for land.

Darkness surrounded me and thirst consumed me. I resisted the temptation to gulp down the saline solution. Salt stung my skin from head to toe. My arms stopped working and calves cramped up.

A big white floaty object slid down the wave almost within my reach. I lunged for it, missed, and got swamped. Down, down, down. I couldn't kick with cramped calves and couldn't pull myself with noodle arms. I closed my eyes and decided to die.

-14-

Day Five

M idnight and the Hideaway kitchen rattled and whistled with steaming pots and pans tended to by the skeleton kitchen crew. Isabelle and staff anticipated the morning after needs brought on by the island's hard core hurricane partiers. Ceiling fans mixed the thick humid air with stovetop aromas. Blue and El Cap opened the swinging door for Isabelle. The trio settled at a small table right inside the door.

"So tell me the rest," Blue softly said.

She stared up, shook her head and handed him the wrinkled cocktail napkin. "Read this."

A puzzled look crossed his face. He unfolded the flimsy paper, gave El Cap a sideways glance then silently read the harried script, his brow furrowed deeper with every passing second.

He stiffly passed the disturbing missive to El Cap.

"There was a, uh, a misunderstanding. "When did she leave?"

Isabelle shrugged.

El Cap looked up, eyebrows arched. "Big misunderstanding, from the sound of this," he emphasized the word big.

Isabelle closed her eyes. "Trouble. All we got's trouble with deep pockets." She let out a deep sigh. "Sirena didn't leave the island and hasn't come back around here." She kept her eyes closed and the words flowing. "Abraham says she never made it to the airport."

Blue scooted from the chair and paced, hands in pockets. "Where the hell is she?" He stopped and looked down at his sister. She wore the face of a woman who aged ten years in ten hours.

She passed a hand across her puffy eyes. "One more thing. Somebody went and ransacked her room."

Tears flowed. "It gets better. Or worse. Lieutenant Inspector Jack paid us a visit with Dragon Lady in tow." She palmed her wet cheeks. "Insisted he check out Sirena's room. Miss High and Mighty lied saying Sirena vandalized the marina."

The men exchanged glances. "They have my camera, hijacked it from Lonnie. What would they want? Her camera?" El Cap asked.

"No idea. Percy has Sirena's camera."

Blue let out a sigh of relief.

"Okay. We're gonna work this out. El Cap and I will regroup, have a bite to eat. Oh, and we'll need to borrow *Sweet Pea*."

"Of course," she said and added, "I'm going, too."

"Well, I need you here. It's safer and if Sirena comes back, you should be the one to take care of her," he said.

Before Isabelle could fuss, he raised a shushing hand. "You rest. I have a feeling we're really going to need your strength and clear head sooner than later."

Blue glanced at his watch. "It'll soon be dawn."

● ● ●

Hurricane Anastasia blew Bimini a wet, sloppy kiss good-bye. Dawn backlit puffy clouds and burned a purple haze across the overcast sky. Thick, salty air made it hard to draw a deep breath. At first light El Cap and Blue motored the dinghy out to where *Sweet Pea* was anchored. Wind gusts hampered the task of pulling anchors, adding time and aggravation to their daunting agenda.

Anchors and dinghy stowed, El Cap keyed the ignition and teased *Sweet Pea's* twin diesels to a slow roar. The engines hummed a throaty tune.

Blue ducked below, safe from the unforgiving wind. His chair squished from liquid humidity. Switching on the marine radio, he attempted to communicate with anyone who'd answer. Nothing came through. His eyes darted upward as he thought he heard El Cap holler.

"What did you say?" he asked as he ventured top side.

"We'll find her when the coconut telegraph is in full swing. We'll find her," El Cap said with a confident nod. "Once all the locals get to gossiping, there'll be accounting for most everyone's status and whereabouts. You know." He shrugged.

"Yeah."

Blue hurried down to make another call. He dialed in and started speaking.

"Mer tribe, mer tribe, come in mer tribe." After a few attempts, Zantae came back. She spoke so softly he mashed the headset to his ear to better hear. She couldn't say one way or another about Sirena's whereabouts.

"I was behind shutters in a meditative state the last two

days and nights. Praise the Lord, looks like it worked." They exchanged pleasantries and signed off.

Blue raised Isabelle on the radio. After hearing her news he went topside.

"What's up?" the captain asked.

"So, I connected with my sister. Jane claims she saw Sirena get picked up by a real big white guy. In a fancy, black SUV."

"Time?"

"Couldn't pin it down. After lunch and before supper's all she remembered."

"Well, Zander took the camera from Lonnie. He drives and virtually kowtows to your lovely ex, her not-so undercover spy. Heard tell this morning some of her other minions were nosing around the marina."

Blue shot a puzzled look. "How you know so much about all these doings?"

Before he got an answer, the boat made a hard turn and Blue hit the deck. The engines were cut to neutral.

"What the hell?"

El Cap yelled back, "Get up here with the hook."

Blue rummaged in the plethora of hastily stowed gear and grabbed a pole with a loop.

"Turtle's all tangled up," El Cap said and pointed. He shook his head at the pole. "Ain't gonna work."

Dropping the useless tool, he dashed below to find the gaff, a pole with a sharp hook. Gaff in hand, he went back up and said, "Pull in real tight."

El Cap snugged the port side to the moving mass of shell,

netting and debris. After a few attempts to hook the mess, he snagged a big hunk of fishing net.

"Ok, ease off," he said.

El Cap inched the boat away from the turtle which pulled the net and its cargo closer. Blue pulled up on the gaff in an attempt to keep the turtle's head above water. Its head raised up and gasped air before it went back under.

He walked toward the aft end of the boat and tugged the heavy load to the swim platform. The boat's incessant rocking hindrance the rescue. Using the power of a four foot wave, he timed the downward thrust and hauled up the debris on the crest. The angry reptile bellied up onto the platform.

El Cap tossed a towel over the turtle's head and then helped guide the victim aboard. Sheer muscles and determination overcame the turtle's fierce resistance.

"Not to worry. We got you, big guy," El Cap said. He pulled out a pocket knife and thumbed it open to saw away the seaweed-infused net from the turtle's front flippers. The towel was knocked off the turtle's head and the captain half gasped, "Oh hell, it's One Eye!"

Blue joined in and helped cut One Eye free from netting. The turtle hissed in protest, pushed away and slid around the deck.

"Look what else the boy got mixed up in." El Cap held up a Rasta colored hair tie. "This was shoved all the way up to his carapace."

Something else fell off the turtle's front flipper. Blue took the hair tie and looked down at the other foreign object.

"Damn if it isn't Sirena's octo bracelet," he said and slipped the bracelet on his wrist.

"Beyond strange," El Cap said. "Still need to get our friend back to sea." They strained to maneuver the hissing turtle, artfully dodging his dangerous beak and vengeful claws. Blue prodded the 200-pound Loggerhead by pushing his backside with the towel.

"Godspeed, One Eye," Blue said and added, "Man, do I wish he could talk."

One Eye belly flopped and disappeared beneath the sudsy sea.

"Where did Sirena meet our underwater emissary?" El Cap said.

The radio squawked. "*Sweet Pea, Sweet Pea,* come in *Sweet Pea.*" It was Isabelle.

Blue ran below when he heard the white noise of the radio. In his haste he knocked over a cigar box. Two cell phones tumbled out. He shot the phones a curious stare as he stuck them back in the box.

"This is *Sweet Pea*, Come in, please."

"Got some news. You know Church Sistah, lives across the canal from my house? One who has the brindle pit? Says the other night she let out the dog to do his bidness. When she steps on the porch to call him home, she saw a white lady running like the devil."

~15~

Day Five

Crippled from intense pain, I sank underwater. Serious thoughts about giving up comforted me for a few seconds. Those thoughts were dismissed when a waterlogged coconut slapped me into fighting mode. Lungs afire, I gave in to my air craving and clawed back to the surface. Barely able to tread, my head bobbed at mere chin level on the sloshing sea. Wham, another knock to the head forced me below. This is it, I thought. Just let go and rest on the bottom. Shaking off the best ideas I'd hatched all day, I hit the surface and faced the latest assault weapon. With shaky hands, I gripped each side of a massive ice chest lid. Laying across the rigid plastic, I finally rested my weary head. Red life flowed from my nose, blood rivulets beaded up and ran off the hard surface. I clutched the makeshift boogie board. Then everything went dark.

Sunshine and lapping waves woke me. Desperate to put distance between me and the sea, I conjured enough energy to raise my arms and when they came down I hit sand. I managed to open one eye. Sand means land.

A big wave hit and pushed me further in. For a brief moment I relaxed in warm sand under the hot sun. My thirst resurfaced with a vengeance. Struggling, I righted myself and then hobbled across a graveyard of seaweed.

Birds circled overhead, screaming, demanding, sizing me up. Buzzing flies and gnats hovered over the seaweed stench, dipping with ease into their smorgasbord. But me, I had to get up and hunt. Dizzy as hell and beyond parched, I set out to forage in a pathetic half-crawl, half-hobble.

Wading through piles of sand blasted storm casualties for sustenance there was everything but clean water. Frayed toothbrushes, mangled bamboo sticks, gnarled mangrove tree roots, broken and intact glass bottles, hundreds of milk jug lids, even toys. Surely in all the trash there was one bottle of fresh water. Vegetation snagged and scratched my bare feet and calves. Thirst rivaled pain. Exhaustion trumped will. Every couple of steps forward, I had to stop, bend over and pant.

I looked down at my body. A ripped t-shirt scarcely covered my upper torso. Touching each swollen arm, I noted the missing watch. Bare hips connected to inflated foreign looking legs sticking out of sad-looking panties.

Drawing a deep breath, I nearly barfed from the stink. A strong sulfur smell lofted, an undertone to the rotten methane odor. Sulfur could mean well water. Injured nose turned skyward to sniff out the source of the horrible, beautiful scent. Following my nose, I stumbled over yet another obstacle and landed on a clearing littered with coconuts. What a tease, so much milk inside and no way to open them. Catching sight of something white, I focused on it, made a slight detour and reached a five-gallon bucket. Coating the bottom was a scant bit of slimy liquid. I cupped a hand and dipped it to my tongue and then devoured it all. When I vomited, the birds swooped down for a swill of my liquid misery.

Heavy head beating a death march, I crawled on all fours attempting to re-discover the sulfur scent. Crawling away from my misery, I dropped face down in the sand and cried until sweet darkness cloaked me.

Awakened by lava hot sun, a deep agony flooded my entire being. I rolled over and winced when something stabbed my back, a bamboo pole. I flopped off of it and grabbed it for a crutch. Pulling up on the strong pole the whole island began to spin. Bent over and gripping the bamboo, I nearly hyperventilated. Lost was the sulfur scent as I concentrated on trying to stand erect. I took another tumble.

Seagulls hollered and swooped on the warm, billowy wind. Splayed out on my aching back, I prayed for somebody to find my ass before the squawking bastards pecked out my very soul. Bird calls morphed to a human voice. When I unscrewed my rusted eyelid, a blurry figure hovered and shadowed me.

"Who? Help…" I whisper-squeaked.

The misty shadow figure laid something cool and wet across my feverish eyes.

"Drink," A woman's voice uttered as she lifted my head. A cup touched my lips and I gulped every single drop. Not water, more like honey tea.

"Keep resting your eyes," she said in a sing-song voice. She changed out the compress for a wetter, cooler one.

"More," I begged and reached out to touch her face. My finger landed on a mole or a scab or a beauty mark. Hearing the luscious liquid fill the cup was a sound so sweet it brought me to sobs. I wrapped my aching hand around hers and the cup.

"Slowly," the angel's voice coached. She stroked my head and the mangled knots that used to be my hair.

• • •

Hollywood Jane's two-man film crew bribed their way onto a small charter plane out of Lauderdale. Being the only passengers onboard, their bundles of gear were guaranteed to stay out of lost and found. They waddled mid-plane and sat opposite aisle of each other, discarding their bulky bundles in empty seats.

"Dude," the larger man, Rik, said. He reached across the aisle to punch his companion on the arm and added, "Money shots, every which way."

Denny, his cohort, rubbed his arm. "Damn, man. I told you stop punching me." He threw Rik a dirty look. He yanked an LA Lakers cap over his eyes, folded his arms across his barrel chest and rolled his head away. He muttered, "Photog ape."

Rik flicked-off his best friend and business partner before he turned away and squinted out the scratched window. His wide grin revealed front teeth sporting gold hemp leaves.

• • •

By late afternoon the sound of progress echoed all around the Hideaway. Large sheets of plywood from outside windows were removed and stored. Teenage boys removed and then folded tarps from the rooftops and boats. Sightseers and Hideaway guests milled around, sloshing through pond size puddles.

Isabelle's worried features contrasted her customers' jovial vibe. She busied herself in the kitchen and jumped each time the land line rang or static roared from the marine radio. She pondered hard over the virtual storm brewing around Sirena.

Jane dove into her lunch at the bar and washed it down with a Kalik.

"Any news on Sirena?" Jane asked Percy between chews.

His eyebrows crawled up his forehead. "Who told you about dat?" he asked.

Jane waved around a home fry. "She got pissed at Blue and took off. Didn't make the plane. Aiden told me she's MIA." She gobbled the fry.

Percy sniffed. "Aiden." He huffed, dried a glass, slid it overhead and added, "I'll let you know."

Jane nodded. "Okay. Thanks."

The double glass doors swung open and Jane swiveled around.

In marched Rik and Denny, looking like a couple of wandering backpackers.

"Jane. Baby," Rik hollered.

He and Denny were loaded down with four foot long rucksacks and each man handled a pair of rolling Pelican cases. They shuffled their massive payloads in Jane's general direction.

Jane looked at Percy. "Three Kaliks, please. And two more plates."

Percy locked eyes with Jane, his annoyance registered by the double wrinkles on his forehead and the slow shake of his head. He rang for a server, ordered the meals and openly gave the men a head-to-toe once over.

The burley men let go of all their stuff and took turns bear hugging Jane.

"Dang, you guys look like hell." She said and pushed at Rik's chest. He sat in her barstool and she turned to Percy. "Judging by appearances, you'd never guess these two are sought-after in the world of film. Got awards and everything."

Percy said, "Good thing they behind the camera." He stressed the word behind and then turned to wait on other customers.

Jane laughed.

Denny replied, "Great to see you, too." His face was fixed in a fake pout.

She motioned for him to sit and shooed Rik out of her chair and into the one next to it.

She whispered, "New development. Got us a missing American. It's hush-hush. We find her and ching-ching."

Rik made a sour face. "Whoa, little camper. Didn't sign up for any Sherlock story. We agreed to film and co-produce an environmental expose. Throw in some post-storm footage for the news junkies. Now we're supposed to hunt down a missing party girl? No can do." He shook his bald head.

"Percy, keep 'em coming," she ordered and shot her crew a dirty look. "Callous as ever. I met the missing woman, Sirena. Not a party chick. She's old, like 40-something. And a Weeki Wachee mermaid who's hung-up on proving ancient Atlantis is on Bimini."

Denny removed his cap and then ran a hand across greasy brown hair. Slapping the hat back on, he replied, "Bull."

"I shit you not," Jane said.

Percy removed the empty bottles and took his sweet time

in wiping condensation from the counter. He flipped three fresh paper coasters and placed uncapped beers on each. Arms braced on the bar, he made no bones about his overt eavesdropping.

Jane continued. "You do know the significance of Bimini Road and Atlantis?"

Denny says, "Yeah more crap. Supposedly it's a part of Atlantis that didn't totally sink or maybe it popped back up. What, a bazillion years ago, give or take? So now you've added Atlantis hocus pocus?" He looked at Rik, "Unbelievable. Does the term shooting script and sticking to schedule mean anything to her?"

Jane dropped her chin to her chest, and then raised her head to shoot daggers at the pair. "Walk if you want. My little black book is full of photo and sound people who can actually smell a story." She folded her arms.

Rik said, "We're here, we'll work the agreed timeframe. Whadda we got to lose, Denny boy?"

Denny shrugged and shook his head. "Whatever. Just tell fill me in on your sources."

"Aiden, charter captain for casino marina. But wait. It gets better. On the environmental side we have tourist Sirena and local hero, Dr. Blue Rolle. They photographed an illegal blast site in the channel by the new marina. Aiden thinks her camera, evidence was stolen. Now she's missing. It's all related."

Rik piped in. "Recap. So we seek out these, uh, reef wreckers. And search for Sirena. Question. This Aiden character, is he credible? And the other cat. Blue Rolle can't be his real name. I mean, it sounds like a sushi dish."

"Irreverent as ever," Jane chided. "Rolle's sister is Isabelle, owns the Hideaway and a big charter boat. They have a pretty good posse searching. No cops so far." She took a beer swig. A bit of light gleamed in her glassy eyes. "Oh, I got a source, all right. Aiden knows a pissed-off marina employee who's ready to spill."

Rik rolled his eyes, "Okay Nancy Drew. Just put it all in the shooting script."

She nodded. "Have I ever let you down?"

"Well, there was the time in Cuba when…" his voice trailed.

"Shut up," she ordered.

~16~

Day Five

Rik opened his mouth to answer but was distracted by a woman. Like a shark on a blood scent, Holly glided in. She eyed the massive packs and the men as she bee-lined to Jane.

"Why, hello, Jane and friends," she said to the newcomers. "I'm Holly." From her back jean pocket, she produced a pair of business cards. "I see I'm not the only one here on business." Handing each man a card, avoiding Aiden's proffered hand, she bent over to Percy, "The usual, Mon."

Holly inserted herself in Jane's cozy circle.

● ● ●

Sweet Pea dodged storm-blown debris in the choppy waterway next to the Hideaway. El Cap steered from high on the tuna tower, Blue was down at the bow. A half-mile up the canal, the boat slowed then drifted to pilings near church sister's bungalow. Blue secured the boat lines to the old pilings best he could.

The men sprinted up and banged on the plywood covered front door. Windows were sealed against the storm in similar fashion. Blue balled his fist and pounded, then switched tactics and hand-slapped the wood.

"Anybody home? It's me, Blue, Sister Isabelle's brother. We need to talk."

Silence returned his efforts. Waves slapped at *Sweet Pea* and the crumbling seawall as distant sounds of power tools disharmonized. Frustration clouded his face and he threw up his arms in an exaggerated shrug. "We'll do a door-to-door canvas, then," he said.

"Ah, let's start with Zantae. She's just a few doors down," El Cap suggested.

Blue motioned for El Cap to lead the way.

Zantae's yellow stucco cottage sported the same makeshift hurricane proofing as church sister's. But her front door was uncovered. El Cap knocked and called her name as he peered through a small diamond shaped window at the top of the door.

"I see her. On the sofa," he said and jabbed the window pane.

"Keep knocking. Wake her up."

"Miss Zantaeeeee…"El Cap shouted over and over. "It's me and Blue, get up, Zantae."

Zantae didn't move a muscle.

"I spoke to her a couple hours ago, I'm sure she's exhausted but…" his voice trailed off. "This isn't right." He jumped off the skinny porch and into the saturated yard. Freeing his shoes from muck, he trudged around and took in the covered windows. He gave a quick glance to the neighbors boarded up homes and saw no signs of life. Zantae's back door was battened. Blue joined El Cap on the front porch.

"Only way in." He pointed at the door.

El Cap said, "Brilliant, we'll do it the hard way." He shoulder rammed the door. It wouldn't give. He stood back and kicked the heavy door until the locks gave and the men gained access, tracking mud across the floor.

Shadowed but for light streaming through the crippled doorway, Blue squinted and kneeled by Zantae as he put a hand on her forehead. El Cap bent down and checked her pulse.

"She's barely breathing," El Cap said.

Blue found a quilt and covered her. He backed up to look at her and tripped on something. Looking down at a wadded up garment saturated with water, he drew closer and smelled sulfur.

"These clothes are soaking wet." He gazed at the garments and picked at them. "What the hell?"

El Cap shrugged. "Doesn't matter right now. Go to her bathroom and see if there's any medication. Look for diabetes or heart meds like nitro." He cocked his head toward the kitchen. "Check in coolers, ice chests, see if there's insulin."

El Cap examined Zantae's face, neck, arms. Her pupils were tiny. Dozens of bites dotted her arms. Gently, he pulled up the hem of her cotton pajama bottom and saw the same marks on her legs and the tattoo of fish scales. He said, "Even with the door wide open, there's no bugs coming inside. No fleas biting me in here, either."

Blue's loud voice startled him. "It's so dark in here, can't read any labels." He gathered two handfuls of small bottles and took them to his waiting friend. El Cap frowned as he read the half dozen amber bottles, opened each, took a sniff and then shook his head. "These aren't prescriptions, the labels are handwritten, all herbs and such."

"Go to the kitchen, cabinets, and refrigerator. Find orange juice or something with natural sugar." He added, "I'll check her bedroom." He returned empty handed and shook his head.

"No insulin." He showed El Cap a bottle of cranberry juice then poured a small portion into a tin cup. El Cap propped Zantae on pillows and gave her face a couple of taps to each side. Her open mouth emitted sounds, incomprehensible whispers. Her jaws worked and lips formed words but they were stuck somewhere between her mind and her voice.

"Miss Zantae, sip this juice. I'm giving it to you now."

He sat her up and gingerly administered the liquid. She swallowed and some dribbled down her face and neck.

"Should we move her? Take her on the boat?"

El Cap shook his head and felt her face with the back of his hand. "Afraid to. She's warmed up a bit but the pulse is faint." He felt above her ankles and shook his head.

"Look at her arms, her legs, something's bitten her. Not an allergic reaction, she can swallow."

Blue looked at the red bumps, the welts.

"Radio mayday for medical assistance," El Cap ordered.

Using the battery-powered radio setting by the front door, he dialed to emergency channel 16 and began his call, forehead wrinkled with worry. A couple of physicians manned two clinics, both on North Bimini. No hospital; it'd be a miracle to get any medical help much less a house call.

The mayday was answered by a woman at the Royal Bahamas police station.

"Doc's out on a call to the Big Bimini Marina. Mr. Jay got a broken leg."

"John at the Big Bimini?"

"Roger."

"So, their radio works?"

"Roger."

"Thanks. Over and out."

"Big Bimini Marina, Big Bimini Marina, come in please."

Static then a voice, "Big Bimini here, go ahead."

Blue relayed the urgent need for Doc to get to Zantae.

"Standby," the deep male voice replied. Seconds stretched to long, silent minutes. When the radio sputtered back to life, the same voice said, "He's on the way."

● ● ●

Early evening and Jane, Rik, Aiden and Denny walked into the Hideaway's near-empty dining hall. They went straight for the bar. The moment he saw them, Percy popped open cold beers.

"To the best barkeep and coldest beer in the world," Denny said and raised the bottle. They all followed suit. "To Percy." They shouted.

Holly sashayed in. "What's all this?" she said.

She slid in the chair beside Rik and gave him a peck on the cheek.

"I thought you made it clear last night, I'm part of your expedition," she said.

Jane was quick to reply. "No. We need to get organized."

Rik tried to soothe over a potential catfight. "The waves are still running three to five, it's more than a little bumpy out there."

"But I volunteered my technical consulting services," Holly said in a sultry voice.

Jane said, "I'm not sure what kind of pillow talk enticed Mr. Wonderful to offer you a job, but I'm the producer, the big kahuna. So he works for me." She paused and looked directly at Holly. "Out of curiosity, exactly what kind of technical consulting are you peddling?"

Holly got up and stood beside Jane. From her back pocket she whipped out a cell phone and pulled a business card from the case. Jane read, Holly von Frost, maritime historian and underwater archaeologist.

"I was part of a dive team that performed surveys on geological formations and sunken structures right off these very shores. Also did my underwater demo training at NASE in Jacksonville. I do believe your team here mentioned they can use my, uh, assets."

"Today's not the day. Perhaps later. I'll let you know," Jane lay the business card in a puddle on the bar, turned to Denny and said, "Now where were we?"

Rik patted the seat next to him. "Let me buy you a beer."

Holly looked calm and cool as she slid over to Rik. Inside she was steaming. She had to get on a boat by tomorrow or else lay a new plan. "I don't drink beer. Percy, you know how I like my drink.

"He nodded and mumbled, "Dark and mean, just like you."

-17-

Day Five

Zantae sat up in the hospital bed, Isabelle by her side. An aide zipped in with a wheelchair. "Here's your chariot, Miz Z." She moved her arms in a flourish and then helped Zantae transfer to the chair.

"Don't you Miz Z me. I don't need any help and I certainly don't need this rolling chair," Zantae said in a scolding tone.

Isabelle gave a few tongue clicks. "Just sit in there until I can get you outside and on your way home." With one hand up, she gave the sign for stay as if training a small child. The trio made their way through the clinic and under the evening sun.

Looking around the aide said, "Where's your ride?"

Pointing to an empty golf cart, Isabelle said, "Right here."

The moment the brakes were engaged on the wheelchair, Zantae sprang out of it, clutching a plastic bag with her name on it. "About time."

"Get in," Isabelle ordered as she slid behind the driver seat. "Huh, be thankful you were in for only a half day. Besides, you owe me an explanation. What the hell happened to you?" She accelerated and Zantae slammed backward into the seat.

"Keep it up and we both goin' back to hospital," Zantae quipped. "Okay I'll explain after you tell me something. Where is Sirena?"

Shaking her head Isabelle replied, "Don't know. Blue and El Cap huntin' for her and so is Jane."

"They'll find her on an islet," Zantae said.

"What? How you know? You still got a little head issue, sistah." The cart decelerated to a low crawl as she veered around a huge mud puddle.

"You know how I know. I got the gift. I saw her. But they better find the gurl soon." She extended her forearms. "Damn bugs tore me up, she's twice as bad and dehydrated to boot."

"Gull, you talking crazy like you always do after one of yo Jesus trances."

Pulling in front of Zantae's house, Isabelle wasted no time in getting inside and to the marine radio. She raised Blue and El Cap.

Isabelle shoved the mic in front of Zantae and said, "Tell them." She pulled out a chair by the radio for her friend to sit.

"All I know is an islet. It had Australian pine trees in the middle and some palms and was full of biting bugs. Oh, and there was a little beach perfect for a skiff to belly in."

Blue bowed his head, "Miz Zantae, you described half the islets around here. Anything else, say north of Alice Town, south of the airport?"

Zantae couldn't say exactly how she'd arrived on the little islet, especially with half the island listening in. The truth would land her back in hospital. This time one for head cases. She hung her head and simply gave it a little shake.

"He can't see yo' head shake, woman." Isabelle keyed up the mic. "It's all she can say right now. I'm tucking her in and heading to the Hideaway. Over."

A fat grin split Aiden's generous lips as he listened in on the radio conversation. His passengers were below deck. "Hey Jane," he hollered, "Get up here."

All three passengers scrambled topside. "What's up?" Jane asked. Aiden shushed her and bobbed his head toward the radio.

His grin widened. "Gentlemen, ready your cameras and strike up the sound. We're about to pull a rescue." Jane planted a smooch on his cheek and ran a hand through her own thick locks.

● ● ●

I called out for the angel lady. Her soothing voice was replaced with bird squawks and the ever present cadence of rolling waves. Elbowing my way to a sitting position, I patted around for more honey water. Beside me was a metal coffee cup half filled with clear liquid. Downing the life-saving fluid, I set down the cup and looked around for the angel and hoped for more to drink. "Angel lady, please come back, don't leave me." My monotone rasp repeated the mantra over and over. Sucking in a long breath, my ears perked to the hum of a boat engine so close it drowned out the chattering birds.

Aiden circled three other islets before he found one with a beach.

"Just like the ole lady said," he shouted to the wind.

Holly grinned as he turned off the engine, sprinted to the bow and let the anchor down. The boat drew too much so he couldn't venture closer to the shallows or the beach. He hurried over to the back of the boat where Holly was poised on the side of the boat dangling finned feet and adjusting her mask.

She pointed to the islet. "I can swim from here to there quicker than you can throw the dinghy overboard. See ya on the island." She splashed into the water and kicked away.

Aiden shrugged. She was right. Before the film crew had gingerly loaded themselves and gear in the dinghy, Holly disappeared from their view as she made tracks on the sandy islet.

Fins tucked under an arm, she stopped to hone in on a beckoning voice.

Jerking the mask under her chin she replied, "Where are you?" Following a raspy voice, she picked her way to the middle of the island and zeroed in on the words, "Here, please, here." No-see-um bugs lit on Holly and covered her skin. She slapped the biting insects and fanned them off her face. Not even blood sucking bastards could keep her from Sirena. After this coup, she was a certain shoo-in for Jane's crew.

Sirena let out a scream and passed out when the men lifted her swollen, beat up body from the sand. She regained consciousness and uttered some words when she was passed from one set of arms to another aboard the dinghy. Onboard the larger vessel, hastily assembled bed made of boat cushions became her bed. Rik grabbed towels and soaked them in fresh water then draped them across her. With care, he laid a saturated towel across her crusty mouth.

"We can give her tiny sips of water not too much at once," he said.

Aiden raced toward the Alice Town clinic while Jane radioed ahead to alert medical personnel. Sirena rocked with every wave the motor vessel hit.

Holly moved the towel and force-fed water until it ran down

Sirena's neck and she gurgled. Rik hurried over and grabbed the water bottle.

"Stop. You trying to kill her or something?"

"Oh, my bad." She walked away and to the cabin. "Toodles."

Denny joined Rik. "Man, we need to put her in the cabin."

"No." She's in a good spot, out of the sun. Just keep soaking the towel and letting the water trickle in. I'm gonna do a little work."

Rik pulled out his camera and took close-ups of the rescued woman. He spun around and took long shots of the islet, the boat and the innocent-looking turquoise sea.

Aiden docked the boat at the makeshift slip in front of the bayside clinic. Denny gingerly cradled Sirena in his arms, her head lolled back and limbs splayed. Aiden tied the boat to the cleat and then jumped up on the dock. Rik assisted Denny in handing their precious cargo to Aiden. A pair of nurses waited on either side of a rolling gurney where Aiden lay her on the cool, white sheets.

Inside the cool building, Sirena's lips moved but no words spilled out. One of the nurses hustled away and brought back ice filled towels and packed them around the fevered patient. Sirena came around and repeatedly hit her arm on the skinny bed. Guttural sounds came from her like a dog fighting for a bone. The nurses leaned in to comfort Sirena. She laid a hand on the arm of a nurse and whispered, "Make them go away."

Sirena managed to keep her hand on the nurse. The older nurse straightened up and assessed the onlookers. Video camera rolling behind the big white guy with a hemp leaf tooth and another one held out a microphone.

"Put that thing away," the older nurse ordered.

Rik complied with a shy, "Yes, ma'am."

"You, too, mister," she laser focused on Denny. He complied. Jane was speechless for once.

"Now all of you stay right here. My patient needs her privacy and some rest." Sirena was rolled three doors down and taken inside a room.

● ● ●

"Hideaway, Hideaway, come in Hideaway," Isabelle slammed the door between the kitchen and the dining room and headed for the radio. She grabbed the mic.

"This is the Hideaway, go ahead."

"Sirena is safe at the Alice Town clinic," Aiden said and shed a little detail on the rescue mission.

Isabelle hung-up and tried to reach Blue. He didn't immediately answer so she hailed the kitchen manager, Suzy. "Don't leave this radio until you let Blue know Sirena is safe at the clinic." And raise Zantae, tell her to get a ride to the clinic and why." Isabelle beelined to the bar and got Percy's attention.

"Praise the Lord, Sirena's alive. None other than Aiden and his charter clowns found her. She's at the Alice Town clinic. Suzy's on the radio, trying to get Blue. She ain't gone stop until she raises him and tells the news. I need to get over there and see Sirena. You in charge." She untied and tossed the apron at him. He smiled and caught it as she rocketed out, leaving him no time to pose any questions.

Blue and El Cap had anchored out from an islet where they

believed they'd find Sirena and swam to the tiny spit of land. They returned to the boat with empty hands and heavy hearts.

"*Sweet Pea, Sweet Pea, come in Sweet Pea. This is the Hideaway.*" Both men dove for the mic. Blue came up with it. Suzy filled them in on Sirena's rescue and whereabouts.

"Fabulous. Brilliant! Who found her?"

Suzy answered, "Aiden."

"She's alive," Blue hollered. He bro hugged his buddy and slapped him on the back.

For the second time in as many days, they were at the clinic's emergency ward. "You again?" the desk clerk said to the men.

"Us again," El Cap replied.

"You checking someone in?" she peered around the water-logged men.

"No. We need to visit someone. Sirena Thomas."

"Your sister and Miz Zantae there already. Room 13. Be careful. Seems the patient has a high temper. She kicked out the very folks what found her and brought her in. Anyway, it's down the hall and to the left," the clerk said and pointed.

The folks who were kicked out stood in the hallway. El Cap spoke first. "Aiden, man, you the hero today." They shook hands. Blue headed over to Rik and Denny to congratulate them.

"What about me?" Jane said as she walked toward the group.

"And you're the heroine, indeed," Blue said and extended his hand to her. She pulled it toward her and circled her arms around him.

"Oh, more like it," she whispered and sashayed over to Aiden. He put a territorial arm around her bare shoulders.

"Well, I need to check on the lady of the hour," Blue said and added, "before I go in, can someone tell me where's Holly?"

-18-

Day Five

Outside the clinic, Holly approached Jane. "I, uh, can't really do hospitals. Bad memories," her voice trailed off. "So I'll hike back to the Hideaway. Ah, speedy recovery to Sirena."

Jane blew cigarette through her nostrils. "Sure, I understand. But one little problem. I doubt the water taxi is running."

Holly half-smiled, "Oh, I've never had a problem hitching a ride."

She couldn't get away fast enough. Thrilled at the golden opportunity to carry out her plan while the others were preoccupied with Sirena. "Too good to be true," she thought.

A young island boy had taken initiative and hauled passengers from one side of the canal to the other in a sad and soggy jon boat. Holly boarded knowing she couldn't pay. As she exited from the aluminum rig, she whispered a hollow promise to bring back the five dollar fare.

At the Hideaway, she caught her reflection in the glass door and fancied herself a mud-wrestling Barbie. Long sleeved shirt was spattered with mud and gunk, dirt freckled her long legs and her dreads resembled octopus arms peering from beneath a bucket hat. She grabbed at the top of the hat and muttered curses, hoping her designer sunglasses were still on the boat.

Peering through to the dining hall she could see Percy tend bar to a packed house. She bolted up the outside stairs and realized she needed keys. She stopped, turned around, and bolted back down.

She slipped to the unoccupied hostess stand where the room keys were kept. Holly helped herself to her extra room key and was reaching for Blue's key when Suzy showed up.

"What happened to you?" Suzy, the kitchen manager, asked. "And what are you taking?"

Holly palmed Blue's key and dangled her own. "Spare key. You got a problem with that?" She stared Suzy down.

Suzy gave her the once over and then put her nose in the air as she bounced away. She pasted a smile on her face when she delivered a large tray of food to a table of six. Holly couldn't get out of there and into the shower fast enough.

Mud-free, she felt bold and invincible, a monomaniac on a mission. Armed with a camera and Blue's key, she slinked to his front door and let herself in. She tiptoed around the flat until she spied a photo album. Snatching it from his dresser she threw it on his bed and shot page after page of astonishing images. After recording a dozen or so pages of the art she allowed herself a moment.

She kissed her Nikonos. "Damn, I'm good."

Holly and her fat ego ended up at the dining hall where she sipped her infamous libation and engaged in her favorite pastime: insult any and all underlings who dare look at her.

Aiden sauntered in and bee lined for Holly. She offered him a sip of her beverage.

"Thanks, I needed that."

"Where's the rest of the crew?"

"Getting cleaned up," he said and added, "Disappointed your little boyfriend isn't here?"

"I have no boyfriend. But I do have cash. I need to charter your boat in the morning.

Aiden cocked his head to one side. "Uh, no? Jane has me sewn up the rest of the week and you're supposed to be the, what is it, tech consult?"

"I'll double your fee. Take me first then come back and do whatever Miss Jane desires."

"So you sleep with a docu-guy to get on board my boat, hoodwink the producer and now you're trying to weasel the charter away from them."

Holly took calming breaths, stood and leaned over him. "Jane got one thing right. Brawn and no brains. I'm sure you'll accept the offer. See ya soon, Gilligan."

She stomped to her room, slammed the door and kicked at air. Shit for brains better take her offer, she had to get out to the cave tomorrow and shoot video starring none other than Holly von Frost. "Beauty and brains, the scholarly diva," she quipped.

An hour passed before she heard a knock. Took him long enough, she thought. "Who is it?"

"It's me."

She snatched open the door and saw Aiden. Sheepish, he held two drinks.

"Peace?" he asked and extended a glass.

"Maybe," she said and ignored the peace offering. She propped beside the open door.

"So I decided to take you up on the offer. I'll just let Jane know the boat needs a part and I have to get it first thing from Cat Cay. Be at the dock at five." He set down the drinks to look at his oversized Seiko and added, "Well, about four hours from now." He sat on the bed. "Jane gives me a grand a day and I give her whatever she wants." He patted the bed.

"Deal. The offer to double died on the table. And you have nothing else I want." A sweep of her hand motioned his dismissal.

-19-

Day Six

Mary Grace slammed the door of her home office. It helped to muffle racket from downstairs. Her pacing stopped as she cracked a grin. The long ebony cigarette holder wiggled as her smile broadened. Bent over a drawer full of folders, she fanned through them with care. The cigarette nearly dropped when she saw a folder containing the sought-after contents on one tiny thumb drive. Desk phone to her ear, her face turned sour and she banged the clunky receiver onto the cradle. "Ridiculous," she screamed. She couldn't risk a conversation over the marine radio and would inform her employer she was in possession of the tiny thumb drive. It wasn't at the marina office after all.

"You'll be safe here," she said as she popped it into her blouse pocket.

High heels clicked on the hallway floor as she strode downstairs into pure mayhem.

She shouted, "Dear God, he's just a bird. With a bird brain. And you are supposed to have a human brain." Bird droppings, feathers and birdseed were scattered on the furniture and the floor. "Clean up this mess. I'll get the bird."

She grabbed a throw cover from the sofa, tossed it over her

bare arm and whistled. "Rosie! Get to here right now," Mary Grace ordered.

Rosie soared toward the skylights of the cathedral ceiling before floating down to his mistress. "Good bird, my baby buoy." Mary Grace said. She puckered her lipstick covered lips into noisy air kisses.

"Open the damn cage."

Frack slipped on debris, recovered and undid the multiple latches outside of Rosie's palatial cage. Frick and Refrigerator didn't budge.

Refrigerator said, "I need to check on the generators, Boss Lady." He bowed and headed toward the kitchen. She called after him, "Tell Zander I'll need him soon."

"Well, don't just stand there. I said clean up this mess," Mary Grace shouted to the twins. She could not and did not care to tell them apart. She stomped away and toward the stairs.

The tune *Rhinestone Cowboy* played. Mary Grace stopped in her tracks. "Whose is that?"

Frack raised a hand like a scolded school boy. "Me. Mine, ma'am." She put out a hand. "Give." He fished in his pants pocket and came out with a Droid, glanced at the screen, and turned off the ring tone.

She punched numbers before hitting the stairs and then cradled the phone between her ear and shoulder. It slid off her slick silk blouse. Cursing as she bent over, she hastily repositioned it on her shoulder on the way to her office.

"Talk to me," she barked into the phone.

Aiden guided the boat to the Hideaway dock where Holly waited under the pre-dawn sky. He pulled the rented boat next to the pilings.

"Welcome aboard. Where we going?"

Holly squirmed out of her backpack and lay it down to unzip a compartment. She pulled out the underwater camera and a piece of paper.

"Hang on, here's the coordinates," she said and handed him a series of digits.

Plugging in numbers, he said, "Bimini Rocks. And you have your super-girl fins," he said and pointed to the monoliths protruding from her pack.

"Yes and you better have the rest of the gear."

He pointed port side with his head to a pair of tanks secured to the rail. Each held a BC and regulator. "Ready to go."

"Good," she said and added, "But there's two sets. You aren't diving."

"If this secret mission is good enough for you to snake a charter from Jane, then lady, I'm all in. And you can't do a damn thing about it."

Holly wanted to push the idiot overboard but played it cool. "We'll see."

While Aiden concentrated on securing the boat to the mooring ball, Holly leaped at the chance to don her gear and lose him before he could cut the engine. He took in her activity for a brief second. Yep, his instincts served him well. She was going in without him. Aiden thought of himself as a lady's man while fellow-islanders referred to him as a parasitic gigolo. To his credit, he was deemed dumb as a fox.

He out foxed the fox in this instance. In an attempt to stand with the BC strapped around her torso, she instead flopped back and slammed onto the bench. Something held her down hard and fast. "You will pay for this, you idiot." She snarled through gritted teeth.

Laughing, he made his way to the deck and sat beside her.

"Now, now, little lady. Let me give you a hand." He applauded and threw back his head in delirious laughter. She shrugged out of her gear and stood to examine the set up.

"You wrapped the bungee cord around the tank neck first. Then you fit the regulator's first stage onto the tank valve. On purpose. You turned on the air so I'd notice it's a full tank. You banked on me not checking how you secured it. Clever."

Still laughing, he turned his back to her and undid his handiwork on his set of gear. Usually bungees are placed on top of the spot where the valve to the reg and pressure gauge fit. Bungee cords are a safety precaution to keep heavy tanks from tumbling out of the racks onto unsuspecting bare feet.

In order to dive, she had to turn off the air and remove the bungee before she could set-up her gear to get off the boat. What Aiden didn't account for was a woman whose raging temper ensured she always won.

He was still chuckling when Holly picked up a ten pound dive weight and beaned the back of his head. She knew she'd have to get rid of him sooner or later. In this case, sooner trumped later. She kicked, pushed and tugged the unconscious man below deck. Using the mask rinse bucket, she doused most of his blood from the deck.

High above the boat flew the red and white diver down flag,

stiff in the wind. Camera gear tucked under the BC and a hand on her face mask, she fell backwards into the sea. She fought the current to stay true to the compass reading. Poor visibility played against her locating the landmark chimney. Fighting the current caused her to consume air at twice her usual rate. With half a tank of air, 1500 psi, she was under the cavern and searching for the secret entry.

After penetrating the cavern and working her way up to the cave and its air pocket, she tossed the lights and camera onto the plateau then pulled herself up.

"Holy Mother of God." She took her eyes off the walls long enough to fiddle with settings and light from the strobes. Switching off the video but not the lights, she attempted to frame up for a still shot. A selfie. "Get a close up, pan slowly up for an establishing shot. Just me and the find of the millennium."

Satisfied the establishing shot would secure her career and social status, she sighed. "More pressing matters up above." With a cavalier toss of her heavy dreads, she pulled on the mask and jumped in hugging the lighted rig tight to her chest. On the surface she inflated the BC, took a compass reading at the boat and dropped back down. She repositioned the camera rig in front of her chest.

Something rammed her side causing her to drop the camera. Flaring her arms and legs skydiver style, the added drag helped to stop and she spun around. With low visibility, a milky eight feet, whatever butted her was out of sight and most likely would recon for a repeat performance. She had to ignore the burst of fear and drop to the bottom to find the camera. Swimming against the current was an air robber so she focused on long inhalations and even longer exhalations. The bright yellow camera lanyard would be easy to spot even in this low viz, she reminded herself. She refused to check the air gauge again until she found the camera.

● ● ●

Mary Grace rotated the phone to her other ear. She stood. "Don't give me excuses. It will be mitigated if you care to remain employed." She punched off and stared at the phone. It rang immediately. She diverted the call, pocketed the phone and went to the stairwell. "Phone boy, get up here."

She handed Frack the phone and said, "You missed a call from Zander. You and your brother go wait for him outside. Now."

Zander drove Frick and Frack to Lucky 13 where he parked in the back. He unlocked a heavy metal door painted with the faded words employees only. Inside, he relocked and then walked the duo to a locker room and pointed out two among dozens. Zander spun around and retreated outside.

Frack said, "Everything is supposed to be in these two lockers. Let's get this over with."

Frick didn't budge.

"Dude, it's a piece of cake. A professional put all the stuff together, all we gotta do is plant it, just like last time," Frack said.

Frick ran a hand through his hair. "Man, bro, last time we didn't have all this crap from the storm floating around. And Boss Lady acting all agra."

"Just one last job and we'll have enough cash to go

wherever we want. Back to Canada, another island, you name it. But not now. Boss Lady got Zander on us to make sure we get the job done. I ain't messing around with that sick asshole." Frack said. They geared up in silence.

Seaweed, dead fish and plastics covered Lucky 13's canal front. Zander pinched his nostrils against the stench as he watched the gear laden Ick Brothers walk toward the water's edge and made sure they jumped in. He stepped inside out of the stink.

"What you doing here?" Zander asked the man in the locker room.

Startled, El Cap shrugged. "You know, just getting something else for the Boss."

"Yeah, she's pretty worked up," Zander said and took a seat in a metal folding chair.

El Cap nodded. "Well, better hustle or she'll have my head." He hurried out, cursing that he'd been seen.

Floating on their backs and kicking out to the designated site, Frick got a chill. "I'm spooked, we could die."

Frack grabbed his brother and shook him, "Bad luck. Never say that. Look, the professionals did all the calculating. It won't go off until later tonight. Besides, any guy with a C-card can do this part. We plant a few seeds in the sea, get out, job's done and everybody's happy."

"You're leaving out the part that goes boom.

• • •

Minutes later Holly's air supply dwindled to nothing.

She surfaced with a curse and put her mouth on the inflate hose to manually fill the BC. Floating high, she dug for the weight pouch, took a two-pounder and then dropped it down the front of her bikini top under dive skins. Considering the dive gear as useless drag, she decided to ditch the empty tank, BC and regulator. She could rely on her excellent free diving skills. On the fifth dive, she spied the camera wedged in a sea fan covered in fire coral and grabbed it as if it were a shiny doubloon.

She broke surface, spit out the snorkel and drew in long, deep breaths. Treading to keep her head above water, she half unzipped the dive skins, groped for and found the weight. After discarding it, she stuck the palm-sized camera in her bikini top.

Head and shoulders now cleared the waterline. Spinning around she spotted the boat on the mooring line. Aiming for the distant vessel, she turbo kicked a couple hundred strokes and then picked up her head.

Something was wrong. It seemed further away. The strong post-storm current combined with an extreme low tide sucked her out and away from the boat. Holly was caught in a wicked current and captive by its infamous cousin, the Devil's Triangle.

$-20-$

Day Six

In uncomfortable silence, Zander drove the Ick brothers the short distance to their flat. Frack appeared relieved as he saw their building. "Man, we didn't think this place would weather the storm. We got lucky, eh?"

Slowly Zander turned around to face them in the back seat. He said, "You lucked out on this one. But I can tell you, Boss Lady's fighting mad. You two better get out of here before the law comes sniffin' around." They bailed out and slammed the car doors.

"Give me the key," Frack said.

His brother nodded, dug out a key and paused, "What did we do to her?"

"Let me put it this way. Her house of cards is starting to cave. So we need to get inside, grab our cash and get our Yankee asses off this island as soon as the airport's open."

• • •

Isabelle sat on one side of Sirena's hospital bed and Zantae graced the other. Blue alternately paced and stopped to gaze at her. Sedated, she lay stone still on her back. Her face was swollen and one eye was patched. She sighed deeply between inhalations. Bags of medicine and hydration solutions dripped through tubes and into fat needles stuck in each arm.

Hums and beeps were punctuated by an occasional high pitched ping in the disinfectant scented room. Nervously twisting the octo bracelet around his wrist, he asked, "Can she hear us?"

Her feet wiggled from under the sheets. As Blue covered them, he noticed lesions on her legs. He looked at Zantae who said, "The Lord delivered her from evil. Praise the Lord."

Isabelle replied, "Amen, Sistah Z." Hands flew across her breast in the sign of the cross and then she continued, "Now when you gonna 'fess up about the rest of the miracle?" She eyed her old friend like a disappointed parent.

Zantae avoided the visual barb by pretending she didn't catch the look. "Oh, it's a bona fide miracle." She began to hum as she rocked her body in a slow back and forth rhythm. Blue caught her on the forward swing and tugged on her long sleeved blouse.

"You have the same marks, bug bites," His voice trailed off as Sirena moaned and rolled her head around on the flattened pillow.

Blue pivoted and took two strides to her side. "Sirena. Thank God."

"Thirsty." I said and then tried to open my eyes but my eyelids wore weights.

Isabelle rushed out the door saying, "Nurse, nurse, we need a nurse."

I heard a cranking, squeaking noise and my torso began to elevate. Someone was moving the bed. I heard liquid filling a glass and lifted my right hand to receive it. Something stuck my arm and kept it from moving around.

"Water," I whispered."

A different voice answered, "Here you go, take little sips."

"More," I said.

She filled another cup. "I'm Nurse Lenora. How you feeling?"

"Wicked headache and my whole face hurts," I said.

Nurse Lenora said slowly, "What do you remember?"

"Scared and thirsty," I said. It hurt to think and was painful to speak.

Nurse Lenora eyed an empty bag. It piggy backed on a larger bag. She said, "We gave you a little something to ease the pain and to rehydrate you," she pointed to the bag and continued, "Do let me know if you need something stronger. Or anything at all. Okay?"

I nodded and realized my left eye was bandaged. "I'm blind?"

Nurse Lenora said, "No honey. We treated an array of cuts, one dangerously close to the pupil. You'll be able to see very soon." She patted my arm and placed a cool cloth on my good eye. I felt her leave my side.

"Dr. Blue, would you step out with me a moment?" Nurse Lenora said.

He followed her through the door and to the nurse's station. He scoured her face for signs of bad news. "As soon as Mrs. Thomas awakens, we are to notify the Royal Police."

Blue stepped back as if the words caused him to move. "Please hold off until she is a bit more coherent."

Nurse Lenora nodded. "Plan to do so. The Inspector who came by, he didn't share the nature of his inquiry." She studied her white banded wrist watch. "I'll check on her again in a half hour, then."

Blue cracked open the door to Sirena's room. "Isabelle, come here a second, please." Her face contorted with worry. On her way out, she shot another serious look at Zantae, who sped up her humming and rocking.

Once in the hallway, Isabelle said, "What's the matter?"

He pulled his sister into a tight hug. "Royal Police wants to question her."

"About how she ended up in the ocean?" She asked and looked up at him, "Or about the visit to her room and the paper he made me take?"

"Both, I'm sure."

Isabelle inhaled and blew out a long stream of air. "How they know she's here?"

Blue gave a slow shrug. "Jane's proud of her heroic rescue."

He motioned for them to re-enter the private room. They stopped short of going in when they heard Zantae. Sounded as if she were whispering a prayer. Isabelle kept the door cracked to eavesdrop and turned her good ear to listen.

Zantae was over the bed, her back to the door. "You had a visitation. Never mind me. It was you who conjured help."

"Wh-what are you saying?" My hand touched her face and felt an imperfection. It felt familiar, a mole or a scar. The door squeaked open. Again. It seemed to be a revolving type.

"Who?" I said. Zantae pulled away from me.

"It's just Isabelle and me. How you feeling?"

"Kinda like Dorothy in Oz," I said.

All three of my visitors chuckled.

"Ah, the humor has resurfaced, a very fine sign," Blue said and added, "Has your memory come back as well?"

My mind careened out of control and anxiety grew with every beat of my heart.

● ● ●

Day Seven

Refrigerator was watching an old boxing match on the kitchen laptop when he heard a bell chime. He paused the action and then swiveled to access a large screen with real time surveillance. He intercomed Boss Lady, "Lieutenant Inspector's here."

"Let him in," she said in a grumpy voice.

Mary Grace tidied her desk before meeting her visitor. She stood at the top of the stairs and waved for the Inspector to come up. As he climbed the stairs, the bird started his antics all over.

"Jack, why didn't you just call?"

She didn't offer for him to sit so he stood with hat in hand. "You need to come to the station and fill out some paperwork."

"Bitch, bitch, bitch," the bird hollered and threw himself around the cage in a juvenile fit.

Mary Grace attempted to reel in her annoyance. She held up one finger to the Lieutenant and walked out to peer over the railing and said, "He hasn't been himself since the storm. Go ahead and give him some more free time."

Refrigerator nodded. "Yes ma'am." He let the bird out of the cage.

She stood in her office doorway. "So, just bring it to me."

"Can't. What I can do is allow your driver to take you over. Meet you there?"

Mary Grace shrugged. "Sure."

He walked downstairs and as he approached the door, did a sideways glance at the bird dancing across the floor. He let himself out.

Rosie strutted across the floor like an Amazon hunter. He'd turn his head from side to side, then march forward, head bouncing like an old hen's. He zeroed in on something and let out a low whistle as he speed walked to a small, colorful object. Using his beak, he explored the item and toyed with the shiny part. He decided it was worth stealing and then flew to his cage. He buried the treasure in his seed bowl.

Refrigerator returned to his boxing match and was startled by Mary Grace's voice. "I thought I told you to let him out."

He stood and said, "I did." He walked behind her to check on the bird when he heard a door shut. He grabbed for his side arm then relaxed when he saw the lawman had let himself out.

"At least your reflexes work," she said and added, "so tell me about this." She pointed to the bird perched in his cage.

"He must've gone back in."

"Excuses, excuses. Get me to the police station."

● ● ●

Mary Grace sat across the desk from the Lieutenant, a

smirk on her perfectly made-up face. She waited for him to speak. Minutes seemed to pass. She broke the silence. "Don't you have documents for me to read?"

"Something like that," he replied. After a pregnant pause he continued. "You see, Mary Grace, there's been another, ummm, incident at the casino marina. Blue and Sirena were in the clinic. Tremendous alibi, by the way."

Mary Grace sucked in a deep breath and pouted a concerned look.

"Incident? Whatever it is, has nothing to do with me. Seems you have me here under, well, false pretenses."

He leaned back in the comfy arm chair and watched his lovely subject squirm in a cheap, plastic chair. "Not at all. I gave you a courtesy call because we need your statement. Tell me everything you know about, shall we say, the quick, spontaneous combustion of the dredge site?"

She rose in a huff and looked down her nose around the small, tidy office. "I have no idea what you're talking about," she sniffed and continued," We are professionals and hold our contractors to the highest standards. I am sure you will discover someone, an environmental radical perhaps, is attempting to frame the casino. Those simpletons will stop at nothing to curtail our construction." She turned and headed for the closed door.

He remained seated and steepled his fingers. "Have it your way. Our divers are in the water investigating. Maybe I shouldn't let you in on this, but I'm sure you, a successful business woman, will understand." He whispered the last sentence, "Marina computers are being borrowed for a bit."

Hand on the door knob, she spoke over her shoulder, "I am

sure your team will get to the bottom of the debacle. This, however, is a waste of my time." She shook her head and closed the door with a bang as the inspector turned off the recording device in his top drawer.

Mary Grace forced herself to walk unhurried and measured. Refrigerator stood and opened the outside door for her and then the sedan's back door. "Where to?" He leaned in to ask.

"Home." she replied. Digging in her purse for a cell phone, she let out a stream of curse words when it failed and tossed the sleek phone across the seat.

● ● ●

Rosie uncaged himself and perched on the ornate molding above the front door. As soon as Zander opened it, the bird flew out. "You little sneak, get back here."

The free bird soared, shiny new toy gripped hard in his pretty yellow beak.

"Sorry, Boss. I'll go fetch him," Zander said.

"No, get Refrigerator to chase him down. You and I are staying overnight on my cabin cruiser. Pack some things and bring your flight bag, Tomorrow we're going on a trip."

-21-

Day Seven

S unrise tinted the sky a deep pewter brushed with strokes of rose. Jane eyed the horizon and then returned to her scowl. She tapped a sandaled foot, checked her watch and then levied stares on her fearless partners Rik and Denny. Her jaw tightened at the sight of them resting under the eaves of the Hideaway. She tossed her cigarette butt in the water and stomped from the boat dock to the snoring duo, resting their heads on a backpack. She hauled off and kicked the backpack so hard it hurt her big toe.

Rik moved his ball cap from his eyes, noted the source of trouble and stuck the hat back over his face.

"Wake up. How can you sleep at a time like this?" she said and pointed to her sleek wrist watch.

Rik pulled his hat further over his eyes. "Easy. Sit down and relax."

"Smart ass," she replied. "You know what I mean. Aiden is more than an hour late. Oh, and your little flavor of the week is MIA, too."

Denny sat up and stretched. "He's on island time and we need to adjust."

Jane glared and said, "Consider yourself adjusted. Now go find me a freaking phone."

Denny flicked her off and moseyed inside. He helped himself to another cup of coffee while his partners trailed him, arguing. They wandered aimlessly around the dining hall like slow pucks in a pinball game. Percy heard them and pushed through the kitchen door, hands gathered in a drying towel. He peered at the noise makers.

"You didn't get enough food the first time 'round?"

Jane said, "No, um yes. These still don't work." She pointed to her cell phone. Aiden's late and we need to contact him."

Percy frowned. "Come on through. We'll use the radio." He bobbed his head toward the kitchen and pushed through the swinging door. He sat in front of the radio and then asked, "Name of the vessel?"

Jane turned a puzzled look to Rik. "Don't ask me, you're in charge of logistics," he said. She stormed out calling for Rik with every footfall.

"What?"

"The charter boat, what's the name?" she said.

Head cocked, he said, "*No Name.*"

"Has to have a name," Jane said.

"Like I said. *No Name.*" Barely able to stifle a grin, he added, "Is the name."

Percy called the boat. After numerous empty replies, he moved from channel 72 to channel 9. Still no answer. Finally, he heard static and a man's voice, "Percy, it's Captain Rod. Switch to six-eight." His deep baritone voice filled the voluminous kitchen.

"Percy, the vessel *No Name* is moored out by Bimini Road.

Just passed it on our way in. Dive flag's displayed. Not a soul topside, far as we could see."

Percy believed the assessment. Rod liked to check out vessels in his hunt for women. He'd flip up his binocs for a quick look. If he spotted dangerous-looking dudes, he'd mind his own business. But when a gang of tourist women was aboard, he'd have his first mate hoist up a pair of panties just below his Jolly Roger flag.

"So *No Name* has no passengers, no captain is visible?"

Captain Rod said, "Affirmative."

"Copy. Over and out," Percy said and immediately raised El Cap.

Jane's face contorted. She snatched off her cap and threw it on the floor. "I paid that weasel in full. I'll break his freaking neck." She stomped the innocent hat.

Rik and Denny were immune to Jane's rants. She usually resorted to bad behavior when things went awry. Percy took in her childish tirade and then said, "Please use our dining room to sort this out."

Rik picked up the crushed cap. Denny tried to usher Jane away from the kitchen and stopped abruptly. In a Columbo-style pose, he said to Percy, "Who actually owns *No Name*?"

Percy's reply was molasses slow. "Lucky 13 Marina."

Overhearing the news, Jane stopped dead in her tracks. "Rat bastard had no intention of setting us up with a whistle-blower. He used my money to charter a damn fine vessel. He's out on a pleasure cruise. With some bimbo." Nervous hands dug cigarettes from her back pack.

"Can't light up here," Rik warned.

"Bite me," she said and bumped hard through the swinging door.

• • •

El Cap tethered his boat aside the one called *No Name*. A red flag with a white slash flapped in the afternoon sea breeze above the vessel; it was adrift. His brow wrinkled as he pondered why it wasn't anchored or tied to the mooring buoy. He shouted for Aiden and Holly as he jumped aboard and then stooped down to inspect an air tank geared up, ready to dive. Pressure gauge indicated the tank was full of air and the gear was clean and dry. Hollering out again, all he heard were waves slapping against the tandem hulls. He slid open the companionway. In the shadowed salon was a body, crumpled and still. Aiden.

El Cap leaped over the steps and jutted a hand to Aiden's pale throat. He detected a feather light pulse and let out a sigh of relief. Looking around the salon, he snatched towels from the chair backs and covered the cold limp body. Blood and body fluids tainted the air and stained the floor of the hot, airless cabin.

"Mayday, Mayday," he shouted in the radio mic. El Cap stressed an urgent need for the immediate dispatch of a boat with a medic. "Alert the police as well" he added.

He radioed the coast guard and carefully reiterated the important news, the missing woman probably had on dive gear. Wearing a BC gave hope she was afloat.

El Cap turned his mind to Aiden. Knowing charter boats

routinely carry oxygen tanks, he scouted for one. He wouldn't move or handle Aiden, fearful of spinal injuries, but he could administer free flowing oxygen. Scouring the vessel for an oxygen bottle, he also opened all the ports to let in fresh air. No O2 tank was found. All he could do was talk to Aiden, urge him to hang on, and hold his cold, ashen hand in his own warm palm. Sounds of approaching vessels caused El Caps' heart to leap.

Aiden was gingerly loaded on the litter and into the swaying boat. El Cap boarded *Sweet Pea* after a young detective interviewed and dismissed him. He motored away for a little detective work of his own.

The tide change caused bigger waves and *Sweet Pea* took them with steady grace. At his destination, he powered down and put the engines in neutral, the boat's drifting shadow cast moving darkness across the shallow seafloor. Visibility was good enough to see outlines of large rocks along the bottom. The sacred site of Bimini Rocks had morphed into a source of pain and fear. Both were reflected across the captain's tight face.

No Name reportedly was moored here. Then adrift. So strange. El Cap knew this is where Holly would dive. Blue confided the sordid news of Holly's snooping and her knowledge of the Atlantis cave art. He made for the mooring line and tied up.

An hour passed and still no sign of Holly and no sight of the coast guard. Several boats loaded with people floated on distant reefs. With binoculars he saw them cast hand lines and grip slanted poles as they angled for fish, their food and survival. Few Biminites owned seaworthy vessels and those who did could barely afford petrol for their own fishing excursions. They pooled resources and fished together.

Locals couldn't afford to form a posse and hunt for a tourist stupid enough to dive alone in unfavorable conditions. But what struck El Cap as highly curious was the blatant absence of marina managers in search of their missing employee and vessel.

Reluctantly, El Cap shoved off of the mooring ball. He needed to prep for tomorrow's charter. A handful of tourists eager to fight mighty billfish paid Isabelle a handsome sum for the excursion.

Motoring toward the Hideaway he caught sight of something bobbing. Diverting course to take a closer look at what appeared to be a giant sponge, he made a slow pass and rested the engines. It was a BC on an air tank. He grabbed a hook and then jockeyed the boat in position so he could snag the gear.

No Name was boldly stamped across the inside of the orange BC. Secured to the tank valve was the first stage with regs and gauges firmly intact. Air pressure was down to zero. Even so, it's a deadly move for a diver in distress to ditch survival gear.

Saving the coordinates, he made another call to the police and then the coast guard, telling both he was sure he found Holly's dive gear. The coast guard relayed some bad news of their own. While enroute to hunt for the missing female, their boat was diverted to a priority, a sinking barge loaded with merchant marines. The Mayday call reported the disaster near Providence Island. However, the radio officer informed him the U.S. Coast Guard agreed to provide backup in the form of a chopper with para jumpers. El Cap was ordered to haul in the recovered evidence and immediately transport it to the Royal Police.

• • •

Nurse Lenora came in my room humming a lively tune and paused long enough to address me. "Good morning. Looks like you had a good breakfast. How you feel?"

She moved my empty breakfast tray to a side table and gave me the once over.

"Fine. Ready to go home."

"Of course you are. Let's get you tidied up a bit." She went to the bathroom, shared with four other clinic guests, and returned with a basin and water."

"I want to shower."

"Not today and don't argue."

Gently she washed my face and arms, the warm water felt so good I almost purred. She picked up a brush and moved toward my hair.

"No," I said and quickly added, "thank-you. Neither of us can do a thing for my hair now. It's ER worthy."

Chuckling, Lenora explained her actions as she pulled one of the IV's from my right arm. What a stinging relief. She gave me a few minutes before lowering the bed with a creaky hand crank close to the floor.

"You get out of bed now," she said and pulled back the covers. "Take your time."

Since the back of the bed was tilted up, all I had to do was rotate a bit so my legs would fall over the side. I managed to sit unaided and flop one leg over the side. My other leg was stuck.

"Damn!" I threw up my hands in disgust and almost fell backward.

Strong arms supported my back. Nurse Lenora steadied me.

"On three, we put other leg over, one two, three…"

Sitting with my sore back hunched over, I dropped my head to my chest.

"You're delusional if you think I can stand, much less walk. Besides, this thing…" I pointed to the IV in my left arm.

She pointed to the rollers on the IV stand. "Not a problem. Okay. Let's get you in the wheelchair first. Then we talk about your hair." She let out a chortle.

Her giggles were contagious. I starting laughing and tried hard to let it out without moving my aching face. With facial muscles fully engaged, my lips and the skin by my eyes cracked and hurt as if fire penetrated open sores.

"Quick I gotta go to the toilet, I gotta pee real bad."

She pointed to the tube between my legs. "Let it go."

I did.

Since the nurse seemed pleased, I took it as a sign to work on my early release plan. I asked, "Since I can get out of bed and have vision in one eye, how about taking out the other IV and removing this from my lady part?" I thought how the mere act of sitting on a toilet unencumbered would be luxurious.

"Sure. But one thing," she said.

"Anything," I replied.

"You must put this under you so I can measure output."

She magically produced what appeared to be a potty training device.

"You're measuring my pee?" I eyed the proffered pee catcher.

She nodded. "You fail to measure then catheter goes back in."

"I'll measure every drop. Now when you gonna spring me?"

She smiled, "Not my decision. Up to Doctor. You ask him tonight when he makes rounds." She smiled and added, "You could use another day but I'll put in a good word for you." She winked and left me sitting in the wheelchair, catheter still intact.

Silence and the room were all mine. Quietness coaxed my ears to relax and prompted my mind to wander. Unsure what day it was, it somehow didn't matter. My thoughts replayed events leading me to the hospital and they seemed more akin to wild imaginings than reality. My heartbeats crescendoed. I rang for the nurse, vowing to raise hell until someone got these body invaders out of me.

-22-

Day Seven

"**B**ut the decal's expired," Zander said as he grabbed his flight bag.

"Your problem, download a paper one when we arrive. Now get the lead out." Mary Grace said then barked, "Meet me at the dock in ten." She dangled a key ring with a float, he reached for it and she snatched it back.

Lucky 13's seaplane was on the tarmac in Cayman Brac with Zander in the pilot's seat. He taxied close to the corporate hangar, conducted post-flight duties and then assisted his only passenger. A man showed up and identified himself, said he'd take care of the plane, refuel and store it in in the hangar. He tossed Zander a set of keys and pointed to a shed where golf carts were juiced-up and ready to go. Zander snagged a cart and drove his passenger to her bayside home.

"Remember, all the locals know me as Miss Rosie Waters," she said. Zander rolled his eyes.

In reality, few people knew her fake name. She was among a growing number of well-heeled foreigners who took a fancy to amenities offered on secluded Cayman Brac.

Like the neighbors, her home set on a half-acre nestled at the end of the runway. She relished the proximity to the airport and corporate hangar. Another perk was keeping track with the comings and goings of private aircraft. She considered this a necessary obsession.

Several times a day, Mary Grace donned a giant straw hat and obscenely expensive Louis V sunnies and walked the beach. Patrolled is a more accurate word since she strung high powered binoculars about her neck and trained her paranoid eyes on overhead traffic.

Even the occasional seafarer who inched close to her shoreline was confronted by Mary Grace, aka Rosie. She wildly gestured and shooed away people who ventured too close for her comfort. Local fishermen avoided angling near her place as did other residents who considered her a crazy woman, possibly possessed.

Mary Grace had to stay put until her lawyer paved the way for her to return home and avoid jail. Sending Lonnie to Jacksonville early had allowed her to transition sans guilt to the Brac. She figured a day such as this would come and was prepared in every way to lay low until pesky details were swept away.

Meanwhile, her modest home wasn't lacking in comfort and amenities. She noticed Zander had helped himself to the whiskey cabinet and food from the well-stocked pantry.

Zander knew he was stuck on the Brac. He managed to make the most of being roomies with Dragon Lady. Her crib was comfortable and he lacked for nothing. He'd been in worse circumstances after other jobs had gone sour. Plus, if things heated up, he had a sweet way out since the plane was within walking distance and he had the only key.

Avoidance was high on Zander's list. His effort to stay away from his hostess was executed with instinct and finesse.

His schedule was the same each day. Right after sunrise, he'd leave the house clutching a mug of tea with breakfast and books in his backpack.

Miss Rosie strolled the beach toward the airport and he took the opposite route. He found Shangri-La when he stumbled on a man-made swimming pool.

The pool in the salty bay was formed by blasting. He marveled to think how dynamite ran him off one island yet created a comfort zone on another. In the 1950's, coral was blasted to form a pool to accommodate divers who lodged cheaply at the long gone Tinker by the Sea Motel.

During times when their paths did cross, she would drill him mercilessly on the use of her new moniker. He could barely keep a straight face when he uttered the absurd persona. Besides, how stupid to call yourself the name of your stupid pet. His one big hope was for her to get discovered. A Nassau jail would be a perfect location for the black-hearted narcissist.

He grew a full beard to match his newest passport. Restless, Zander devised a plan to ditch Mary Grace, the ultimate double-crosser. One night just before dawn, he fast-pedaled a bike to the Lucky 13 hanger. He commandeered the single engine plane, fueled and ready to fly. His flight plan indicated the destination as Bimini. But his course took him to Cuba where partner in crime, Refrigerator, patiently waited.

● ● ●

Someone strode into my dark room.

"Come in," I said in a sarcastic tone.

A man in a white lab jacket looked at me over a clipboard clutched at eye level.

"Thank you," he said and flipped a page. He added, "I'm Doctor Maharaj." He checked my wristband and then produced a pen light from his front pocket. He shined it in my eye.

"What's your name?" he said.

"Audrey Hepburn." My quip garnered the rise of one salt and pepper eyebrow.

"Your eye looks good. Now I shall remove the bandage from the other."

Gently he pulled off the gauze and then an eye cup. I flinched when he pulled off the tape. He patted my shoulder. "Can you open?"

Still covered in a layer of creamy salve, it opened but my vision was blurred.

"Wipe this stuff off so I can focus," I snapped.

"The nurse will bathe your eyes and face. Let me take a look." He attacked me with the bright pen light again. "Hum, dilating nicely. Good."

Pocketing the light he traded it for the stethoscope around his neck and put it to work. "Breathe deeply, please." He put it on my chest. "Okay. Sit up and swing your legs to the bedside."

All these orders and I haven't had a chance to barb him about his last name. Maharaj.

Glad I'd practiced earlier, I slowly complied.

"Good." He put the scope to my back and ordered, "Breathe deeply."

He listened for a half dozen breaths then looked at me. "What are your chief concerns?"

"Going home. Today."

He smiled and flipped through my chart as if hunting for an answer.

"Can you stand?"

"Sure," I lied.

He swept an unencumbered arm, a sign for me to stand. With slow precision I began to slide off the bed, feeling the cool sheets across my bare bottom. Upright, I gripped the bed to steady myself and flinched with pain.

"See." I said and then immediately sat down.

"Go where? Who will care for you? I understand you are an American tourist."

"Makes me sound like a piece of luggage." That got a grin out of the middle-aged medicine man.

"Answer my questions, please."

"Friends. Isabelle and Dr. Blue Rolle."

He nodded. "We've pumped you full of fluids to combat dehydration. I'm pleased with your input and output measures." He paused. "On a scale of one to ten rate any pain you're experiencing."

Afraid to admit it, I shrugged and tilted my head side to side as if undecided.

"The cuts and abrasions, contusions must be painful. But they shall heal. Currently we administer a simple pain reliever every six hours. Do you need more?" He went into a lot of medical jargon about my condition. All I cared about was getting out of there fast.

"About your release. When able to walk around this room on your own legs, even if assisted, you may be discharged."

"Watch." I slid off the bed again. I managed to put one foot in front of the other before the bottoms of my scabbed feet shot pain up my legs. I grabbed the bedside table, straightened up and attempted a smile.

"Around the room and a nurse must witness the event."

"Hardass," I muttered under my breath and stumbled backward to find the bed.

~ 23 ~

Day Seven

C haos and humidity ruled the day inside South Bimini's re-
opened airport. Posted departure times offered a glimmer
of hope for the throngs of people aching to fly home. Repeated
announcements summoned folks holding tickets for Bahamas
Airway to display them as they proceeded to the head of the
lines. Other major airlines were expected to be in service in a
day. Maybe two. Individuals seeking to purchase tickets were in-
structed to sign up on clipboards provided by agents at the counter. Both the air conditioning and patience had failed. Giant floor
fans buzzed and oscillated hot air around the overcrowded lobby.

Royal Bahamas Police Force officers patrolled in twos
while a serious-looking pair stood behind each ticket counter
next to tired-looking clerks and indifferent bag tenders. No cus-
toms officers were in sight.

Frick and Frack were stuck in a stagnant line along with
hundreds of other harried visitors bent on going home. The Ick
brothers had far more at stake than the tourists who pressed
around them.

Their involvement with Lucky 13's shortcuts, the corporate
term for getting a job done illegally, could be hard to prove. But
the gun brandishing stunts were worthy of prison time since
gun possession was prohibited on the island.

Scanning the crowd, Frick said, "I bet those ass wipes took off from Cat Cay."

Cat Cay, a private island close to Bimini, sports an impressive private runway. It's where the casino owners keep a hangar with a couple of planes fueled and setting on ready. Same for a handful of go-fast boats kept at the casino marina. Anybody need or want to get away quick and unnoticed could execute their plan in a heartbeat ahead of the police or irate lovers.

"Yeah. After we went and did those jobs not a one of the bosses offered us a safe way off this hellhole," Frack said and added, "Listen, we get caught, we freakin' sing. Otherwise, we'll end up under a Nassau jail."

Frick nodded and jerked his head to the cops. "They're starting to freak me out."

"We'll be all right. Got their hands full keeping the crowd under control." He gave a dismissive turn of the hand. "Here's what I'm thinking, we can use some cash to buy our way up to the head of the queue."

"What are you talking about?"

"How many people are in front of us right now? Fifty? Sixty?"

"Give or take."

"And once all the ticket holders get taken care of, we'll be closer to the Air Bahamas clerk, right?"

"Right."

"If anyone in front of us buys a Bahamas Air ticket to anywhere, we start handing out cash to get to the clerk. We can't afford to let the last seat get sold right in front of us. We shouldn't be here another hour much less another whole day. Get it? Offer the people in front of us fifty bucks to cut in line."

"These folks got money or they wouldn't be here. Fifty ain't crap to them."

"We can sweeten the pot," Frack said.

A commotion near the doors caused a hush to fall over the airport crowd. A man wearing the summer whites of Royal Bahamas police made a grand entrance. But his wingmen were cause for the crowd to turn stoic. A dozen or so heavily armed men followed the overdressed officer. They guarded all exits and surveyed the room, eyes dared anyone to misbehave.

An intercom voice boomed, "Everyone remain calm and in your place. Produce your passports now and display to the officer who approaches you."

"We're screwed," Frick said.

Two female officers flushed out people who were in the ladies' restroom and a pair of male officers performed the same task in the men's room.

A brazen American-sounding woman questioned the officer who inspected her credentials, "What's going on? You're holding up progress here."

"Ma'am, just stay in line and let us proceed without resistance."

Her traveling companion elbowed her saying, "Shut up, we aren't exactly in Kansas, Toto."

When Frick and Frack were asked to display their credentials, Frick hesitated. He patted first his shirt pocket and then his pants pocket. "Man, I must've left my passport at the flat. Let me go get it."

His brother nodded. "Yeah, me, too."

The officer didn't bother breaking into a knowing grin. In a flat monotone he said, "But of course. I have someone who will be happy to drive you."

Frack replied in a trembling voice, "No, we can walk."

A male cop appeared along with the Lieutenant. The passport check continued as the pair were escorted outside.

● ● ●

The Ick brothers sang two part harmony. Lt. Jack seemed satisfied, armed with a short list of names and a long list of dirty deeds. The story of Mary Grace wanting Sirena silenced caused a look of enlightenment to spread across his broad face.

Lt. Jack showed up at the clinic and was escorted to Sirena's room by a fast walking, grumpy charge nurse.

"Experience has taught us to reserve several exam rooms for inpatients. This storm has produced three requiring an overnight stay. Mrs. Thomas among them," she explained.

"Do provide names of the others as well. You may give them to the officer waiting at the triage desk. As soon as possible."

The nurse nodded and simultaneously knocked on a closed door.

From a deep sleep, I awoke with a gasp. A quick thought of my Atlantis dream teased my memory. I didn't bother to address the knocker. Medical types usually gave one loud bump on the door and then simultaneously charged in. The bedside light flicked on.

Blinking the light and goo from my eyes, I attempted to focus.

"Mrs. Thomas, I am the charge nurse and this is Inspector Lieutenant Jack with the Royal Bahamas Police Force. He is deputy in charge of the North and South Bimini stations. If you are feeling well enough, he would like to ask you some questions."

With a shrug I said, "Sure."

The big cop removed his hat and held it in front of his very white uniform. "Good evening, Mrs. Thomas. Pardon me for waking you. There is a pressing matter at hand. I believe you can assist us."

"I'll try."

The charge nurse crossed her arms in front of her chest, shot him a sideways glance. She glanced at her wristwatch.

"If you have other duties, please don't let me hold you up," he clipped.

"Not at all, sir. I shall stay with my patient."

Grateful to have a witness, for what I was unsure, I cracked a half smile in her direction.

"Mrs. Thomas, how did you end up on the islet?"

"Well, one minute I was on a seawall and the next in the drink." Being a poor girl raised in the south, I knew when cops asked questions, we answer short and sweet.

He wore a face of pure stone. "Seawall, you say. Where?"

"Umm, not sure."

The nurse interjected, "Her head injury..."

"Unless otherwise addressed, kindly do not answer," he said in a voice as cold as his face.

With a long inhalation, she drew up tall and squinted her eyes.

"Come now, Mrs. Thomas. Surely you know where you made the fateful step into the sea. Or were you shoved?"

"Shoved?"

"Where did you enter the water?"

"Airport. Tried to get out ahead of the storm."

"You fell in the water at the airport?"

I grabbed the water glass and took a long swig. This isn't how I want to recall the hell between leaving the Hideaway and looking into…

"I'm having a hard time recalling." I coughed for emphasis.

Charge nurse said, "While you haven't addressed me, I am addressing you. Please leave and do not return until a physician clears you." She strode to the door, opened it and made a sweeping motion with her arm. Lt. Jack didn't budge.

"Page the good doctor. Now. Tell him police business dictates this woman answer my questions."

"Pager system down. Remember we had a little storm? While I am sure Mrs. Thomas will cooperate with you in due time, now is not the time. So please do produce a warrant or leave. Sir."

The attack nurse helped me stall until we could summon Isabelle and Blue. They had to be present during future interviews. He knew my near-drowning was no accident. But was he trying to find the bad guys or was he on a mission for them?

"I'm sorry. My head, my throat. So tired," I said in a pitiful whimper.

Pushing his angry face closer, he bent over me and said, "Do get better. I shall see you in the morning. Bright and early." He stood and added, "Nurse, be advised an officer will be stationed outside this doorway." He yanked open the door and rushed out, closely tailed by a subordinate.

"Thank you," I said to the nurse.

She checked my speeding pulse and fussed, "Not to worry. Oh Lt. Jack, he think he owns us. Come in here all puffed up, throw his weight around. He grills my patient with a head injury." She shook her head and harrumphed.

She drew a breath and let it out when she fluffed my pillow. I figured her tirade was over. But she got a second wind. "I know with all the storm troubles going on, they's something serious what happened to you. Seems you managed to get out of one kind of undercurrent and right smack into another."

$-24-$

Day Eight

Inspector Jack posted a young constable outside of Sirena's room, as much for her protection as a show of his authority. He needed to nail the connection between Sirena's room getting tossed, her going missing and what role, if any, Mary Grace's company played. Sirena was close to the Rolle family and there was a slim chance she wouldn't speak against Blue's ex.

Blue and Isabelle hopped the eleven o'clock ferry to the uptown clinic. Once in the hallway and nearly to her room, they could see someone seated outside Sirena's door, arms folded and hat pulled low on his face.

Blue picked up his pace. "Excuse me, sir, is Mrs. Thomas all right?"

The guard, wearing a Royal Police uniform, jumped up and studied the pair. "No visitors allowed."

Isabelle put a hand on the door. "You can't keep me out."

Clearly, the constable didn't want to put his hands on a respected elder, a pillar of his community. Yet his high superior had made it clear, only medical personnel allowed. Isabelle spoke in a chiding voice, "Young man, don't look at me in that tone of voice. I know your grandmother!" She pushed her way in. The cop hung back and eyed Blue.

Blue spit out questions. "Was there a security problem? Why's a guard on this patient?"

"Sir, only medical personnel are to enter this room. Those are my orders."

Very slowly, Blue withdrew his wallet from his back pants pocket. He fished out an identification card inked with his title.

"I am a doctor."

The young official was well acquainted with most of the Rolle family members. He could explain Dr. Rolle's presence in the patient's room. But Miss Isabelle was going to be a tough sell. A conflicted look crossed the cop's boyish features.

Isabelle wasted no time in delivering her message in a fast, staccato monologue. She told of the inspector examining Sirena's room after it was tossed and mentioned Mary Grace's presence.

"The inspector left this for you to sign," Isabelle said and handed over the paper.

When the door swung open again, I jammed the document under the bedsheet and Isabelle stopped mid-sentence. We looked toward the door.

"Tis only me."

I pulled up the sheet higher on my chest and then sucked in a long breath. I exhaled and quickly told of the inspector's bedside visit. I said, "Does the cop plan to protect me or arrest me on trumped up charges?" I dug out and scanned the document. "My vision's still blurry. What does it say? What's all this mean? I handed it back to Isabelle.

She held the paper and gave me the gist. "Until you produce evidence of the marina blast, you may not leave the island."

She shook her head. "Dragon Lady got the evidence and we'll never see it again."

"No we won't. But isn't my punishment a joke? I mean getting stuck on Bimini."

Blue took the document and looked it over." "Doesn't state anything about detainment."

"You mean jail?" I asked.

He shrugged and said, "Doubt he'll arrest you. We got a little insight last night from Abraham. Yesterday when he drove tourists to the airport, the Ick brothers got arrested there. Our favorite Inspector hauled them in."

Isabelle said, "We'll see what those weasels come up with." She turned to me and shook a forefinger in mock scolding, "Huh, you get stuck here and we'll put you to work. I'll have the only charter with a mermaid deck hand."

Laughs and chortles filled the antiseptic room. When we quieted down, Isabelle spoke.

"You need to know some more tings. Yesterday all kind of doings. Seems ole Dragon Lady up and left. Her bird showed up at the Hideaway and Percy went to take the little varmint back. He say dat place locked up tighter than a drum. We stuck with the feathered one now. I called Lonnie. Her mother's not at the Jacksonville house either. So our sweet girl be coming home tomorrow."

All this information laid on the surface of my mind, slow to mingle with what I knew as truths. My castle in the sea, one fleeting glimpse of a goal met and I'm punished. Cursed. Drowning with my dream, drowning in a maelstrom of greed and deception.

"Your turn, Sirena," he said.

"Oh, tell me more about Lonnie."

Blue shot me a look. "Later. Tell us what happened. To you."

I spit it all out. Verbal diarrhea. "Photographing the blast site is what landed me here. Surely they don't know about the other. Frick and Frack deserve to get arrested. They chased me down after I managed to escape from the little house, the one Mary Grace's goon took me to."

Blue settled his gaze on me. Isabelle took backward steps and fell into the chair. Their slack jaws registered incredulity.

"The Ick brothers chased me to a seawall and pulled guns. I avoided them by jumping in the water." I poured out the rest of the story and in the midst of my surreal recitation, an altercation in the hallway caused me to stop. Wide-eyed, we strained to listen. In a half minute, Inspector Jack hurried in, glancing at his watch.

"Well, good morning, what's left of it, Mrs. Thomas. And to Miss Rolle and Dr. Rolle, I bid you a good morning and a quick farewell."

Isabelle hadn't moved a muscle. She said, "I'm going nowhere."

The inspector pulled open the door and ordered, "Come in here, now."

A new constable rushed in and stopped beside his superior.

"Show these people out. Hold them in the lobby until further orders."

In a deliberate gait, Blue crossed to his sister and took her arm in his. "We'll go on our own accord, thank you."

With all three gone at the Inspector's whim I had to be cautious of his ability and opportunity to misuse power.

"Mrs. Thomas, good to see you're on a quick mend. Now, with the return of your facilities, I'd like to have a little chat with you this morning. May I?" He pulled a straight back chair to my bedside.

"Yes, you may sit. I'll answer your questions best I can. Go ahead." I hoped someone with my lunch tray would pop in real soon.

"Did Miss Rolle deliver the document I left for you?

I nodded.

"Very well. Any questions?"

Shaking my head no, I bit my tongue to keep wise cracks in my head.

"Why did you take photographs near the casino marina docks?"

Here we go. I took in a deep breath. "Because I believed the area was illegally blasted in order to deepen the channel."

"What gave you the idea?"

I paused. "Uhh. I was scuba diving. There was a blast. My happy ass almost got killed from debris hitting me and it got real personal. Rumors flew so I decided to see for myself." I shrugged.

"You snorkeled at midnight where you highly suspected a blast had occurred?"

I nodded.

"Where are the photos from your mission?" He mockingly used the word mission.

"Not sure. A marina security guard stole my camera."

"You can give me a name or a description of this employee? And, I understand the camera was returned."

I shrugged.

"During your visits to Bimini, you always stay at Isabelle's Hideaway. Ever get your room tossed before? Because someone did a real thorough job."

"Never."

"Who would ransack a tourist's motel room? Someone looking for something. Your camera. Was it stolen?"

"You tell me. I haven't been there nor inventoried my belongings since I was, umm, inconvenienced on your lovely island."

"Speaking of which. How did you end up in the sea during such a storm? And live to tell of it?"

Crap, I led him right into this one. "Ahh, it's all kind of fuzzy to me, really." He folded his arms and sat back in the chair. He challenged me with a look of determination.

So I gathered my energy and told the big asshole the truth. Except for the parts about One Eye and Zantae. I kept those fantastic tidbits to myself.

The revolving door was pushed open by a young woman who delivered my lunch. The inspector had to move so the tray could get repositioned over my bed. I thanked her as she removed the plate cover to reveal my fare.

"Before you go, can you let the duty nurse know I need her services?" I cut my eyes to the uniformed cop across the room and back to her, trying to relay a pleading look.

After a series of quick nods, she left the room.

"Perhaps, Inspector, if I'm not kept from real nourishment,

my memory may return," I propped up the metal fork in one fist, spoon in the other and cocked a half smile.

"Bon Appetite, Mrs. Thomas. We shall resume at a later hour." He stopped at the damn overused door and added, "Please understand should I interrupt your afternoon tea."

He spun out and left the door ajar. It'd need new hinges after my brief stay. Heavy footfalls on the terrazzo floor faded and a light footed woman strode in. Nurse Lenora.

I verbally grabbed the woman. "Did you see the Rolles?"

"They in the waiting room along with the constable and now the inspector."

"You gotta get me out of here now. Please dismiss me."

She took my hand and said, "You stirred up some deep current on this island, and could be a might safer in here than out there."

"I didn't stir up anything, I merely held a light to it."

"And seems you fixin' to get burned from all that good light. Only Dr. Maharaj can dismiss and you know what to do."

I slipped off the side of the bed, nourished with two bites of real food and enough chutzpah to get me around the room.

She took my arm under hers and we shuffled round the tiny space. My legs were wobbly but my will was strong. After my victory lap, she settled me in the comfy chair. I looked up at her and thanked her through my tears. Even the bad eye cried.

~ 25 ~

Day Nine

Lonnie returned to the Hideaway in time for the afternoon homecoming.

"Welcome home, I'm so grateful you're all right," Lonnie said as she hugged me.

Blue gave her a quick peck on the cheek and resumed escorting me through the Hideaway lobby. Lonnie locked arms with Isabelle and they led the room of well-wishers in a round of applause and a rowdy *For She's a Jolly Good Fellow*. This good fellow nearly passed out and video cameras seized every unflattering second.

Through a fake smile and clenched teeth I uttered, "Get me to my room."

We wasted no time hobbling to my new room closer to Blue's flat. It was far more orderly than the thoughts swirling in my head. One thing still needed straightened, I thought while getting settled in a cushy chair.

"So, why was Jane in your room that night?"

He pulled up an ottoman and settled my sore, bandaged feet on it and then sat across from me. "She let herself in, sat down and grabbed for the album. But I got to it first. She doesn't know and there's no way I'd ever tell her anything." He hesitated then said, "You doubting me was almost as painful as how

I felt when you were missing." His serious face matched my own somber mug.

Trouble always follows when emotions take power over my actions. A knee-jerk reaction got me in trouble at the marina and didn't help when I ran away from Blue. Now the cops are paying me unwanted attention and the bad guys probably have a fat bounty on my head.

"I'm sorry for my stubbornness about the marina. It was unfair to you. Hindsight? I'd prefer to get to know you in an entirely different way. And though hard to admit, the Jane thing was part green-eyed monster."

After a long, uncomfortable silence he said, "Accepted," and added, "May I have a redo?"

He's asking me for a redo? Should be the other way around. I nodded and put out a hand. "Redo me."

"Like this?" He pulled my hand to his heart and leaned in to me. He brushed feather kisses across my lips and then kissed his way up to my eyes and back down to my lips.

Pulling back, we locked eyes. What a kiss. His eyes pierced my resolve and made me dizzy.

"If only a kiss could erase my other blunders, I'd even kiss up to the Inspector."

With a chuckle, he sat back. The joy in his eyes faded.

"What's wrong? You know I was joking about the cop stuff."

"Indeed. There's another issue. We have a loose cannon, so to speak. Do you recall Holly, she was with Jane and all on your rescue?"

Nodding, I conjured her image, how she appeared to me on the islet, a savior. But Blue's careful words repainted her image with broad strokes of greed and deception.

"Oh hell no. Jane's in on it too? Paid off by this rich bitch who rode in on your coat-tails? The whole freakin' lot of them will go straight to the press and Bimini will be decimated from within and without."

"Let's cool our emotions."

He pointed to a pitcher of water, poured us each a glass and we sipped. Acid clawed at my throat like a provoked crab.

"Not Jane. Aiden. He has the reputation of a shady player and leans whichever way the wind blows."

"So who's keeping an eye on those Judases?"

"Holly, well, she's missing. Aiden's in hospital, he's in bad shape."

Choking back rising bile, I stood too quickly and immediately sat down. Wildly gesturing like a maniac, I spat out my two cents.

"Evil bitch could be stateside or in Nassau, showing, even selling, images of the cave art and God knows what else. But on this island the esteemed Lieutenant Inspector Jack is breathing down my neck instead of sending out a posse to look for a missing person?"

"The Royal Coast Guard is based out of Nassau and doing their best. The other bit is Aiden chartered from the casino marina." He put up a hand. "Yes, them. Again."

● ● ●

Late afternoon, Inspector Jack made an unannounced appearance. He went straight to Blue's flat and spent twenty minutes grilling him.

Pushing back from the dining table he continued, "Dr. Rolle, I understand Mary Grace is the mother of your child, but she's truly the crux of our investigation. We need to find and apprehend her. So you will give me a list of her possible whereabouts." He pointed to a wall clock. "By the day's end."

Watching the Inspector leave, he said, "Then why did you let her get away in the first place? She was in your office."

"She'd be dead if I let her stay, even inside the jail. We see the big picture now, we seized and studied her work and home computers. Those players she's messing with are way out of her league. She has a choice. Either she's for them or against them. If she's against them, we have a plan to keep her safe." He let himself out.

Mary Grace was manipulative, a piss-poor mother and infamous for her shady deals but he didn't want her dead. What he wanted was for her to be found alive and do the right thing. For once.

Isabelle walked in. "I saw the big Inspector on my way up. He was in a rush. What he told you?"

Blue motioned for her to sit while he put on a kettle.

"I have to give a list of possible whereabouts for Mary Grace."

"Nobody knows where her hidey hole is, nobody gonna talk if they did."

He waited for the kettle to boil. "Except Frick and Frack. They're still alive in custody, last I heard."

"She don't tell those hammerheads the time of day, much less where she gone run to."

He set the teapot in front of his sister. She poured and said, "Lonnie may know something she doesn't know."

"Huh?"

"She may know something seems to be nothing but turns out to be serious something. What if she overheard talk of new property or a house needs decorating? Mary Grace may be in a hidey-hole, but you know she'd never sacrifice comfort for anything or anybody."

"So who asks Lonnie? You or me?"

"Me. Once she's settled this evening." She glanced at her watch. "Wonder if Sirena overheard anything about ole Dragon Lady from those kidnapper goons?"

He crossed to the kitchen and put his cup in the sink. "I told the inspector she was resting. I'm sure he's after the same information. I'll go down the hall and check on her."

A few knocks on Sirena's door and no answer. He called for her. Nothing. He tried the door. It was unlocked and he went inside, calling her name.

On the table was a note, "Downstairs, got stir-crazy." He left the note and locked the door on his way out. "Can't believe she didn't lock the door," he mumbled.

Taking the stairs two at a time, he hurried into the main hall where he saw Rosie in a bird cage in a corner and Sirena sitting next to him.

"Once my tormentor, now my fine-feathered friend. Rosie even whispered a few secrets. Says you put him in a tiny house and barely feed him," I said to Blue.

"You believe the little devil?" he said and added, "This tiny house downstairs is the best we could do since Rosie flew away from his mansion. His perch at your flat isn't too shabby, either. And look, he has plenty of food."

We both peered into the cage with all sizes and shapes of seeds scattered across the bottom of the cage and a near-empty food tray. "Well, I filled it up this morning." He opened the door and pulled out the tray.

"Hang on to this, I'll go behind the bar and get him a refill."

"We're talking bird food, not alcohol."

Waiting on him to return, I decided the tray needed cleaning and dumped the old seeds in the ashtray. Something silver and about an inch long spilled out with the soggy seeds.

$-26-$

Day Nine

B lue's eyes nearly bulged when he saw the memory card.
He said, "Let's move this party upstairs."

He powered on the laptop and stuck the memory stick in. Numbers danced across twin screens and Blue's face glowed from its light. "Powerful," he uttered. "Records of purchases and payments from a bank in Cayman."

"Do we show this to the Inspector?"

"Not yet. There's a lot of memory on here and it's full. I'll be up all night."

"Make a copy before you do anything else."

"Indeed." Blue rummaged around in his desk drawer. "I copied to my pc but don't seem to have an empty stick. This thing's one gigabyte. I'll have to go out to Alice Town tomorrow. You hang on to this." He handed over the card.

Without a pocket or purse to stash the priceless nugget, I stuck it in my bra.

"You know what this means?"

"Yeah, Mary Grace goes to the slammer."

"Perhaps. We could have may have solid proof of who purchased blasting materiels and paid professionals to assemble and plant explosives. The irony of it all. Rosie is the only living thing Mary Grace loves almost as much as she loves herself."

"We may have the means to stop the dredging and put the bad guys behind bars."

"Exactly," he said.

"So why the hell did Mr. Inspector let her go? As your sister would say, 'they a fox in the hen house.'"

A hard knock at his door sent us both on alert like a couple of guilty teenagers. I grabbed my chest with both hands. "Crap, should I hide?"

He raised his eyebrows and put a forefinger to his lips. "Yes?"

"Me, just me," El Cap said.

I blew out a loud tone as Blue let him in. He looked like hell. For an instant I thought he'd been in a fight. He said his hellos and took a seat. Blue fetched him a cool drink and said, "What's up, man? You look rather, um, raw."

El Cap removed his trademark Greek Captain's hat and laid it beside him. He ran a hand up his sweaty brow and back across his thick hair. He massaged the back of his neck.

"Where to start?" he said and added, "Short version, I was out on *Sweet Pea* all day then cleaned and refueled her. Loaded up bait, food and poles for my morning charter. And some other crazy stuff. Long day." He took a long swig.

"You can shower here, man," Blue offered.

"Thanks. So you heard about Aiden and all?"

I broke the silence and said what we probably all thought, "We heard. And can't say I'm all shook up."

Blue cut his eyes at me and El Cap took in a deep breath.

"Cut the pretenses. If she's never found, it's best for the whole island," I said.

"Coarse words, Sirena." Blue said and then looked at El Cap, "Did you check the gear? Where is it now?"

"No camera. Just the BC and tank, reg and gauges. Handed it all over to the Royal Police."

"She comes back and nothing can stop her from spilling her guts, telling everyone she found a link to Atlantis all on her own," I said.

El Cap said, "It was your goal to find it, too."

"Damn that stung." I crossed my arms and remembered the golden nugget nestled next to my skin. "You both know I had no intention of crowing over any discovery. Else I wouldn't be here right now."

El Cap blushed. "Apologies. I know you aren't cut from the same cloth as Holly. Another hard truth is the search party won't quit until they find her."

"And to think, I had to rely on an angel and a team of greedy misfits."

Both men eyed me.

El Cap said, "We need to determine how to carry on if or when she resurfaces with her incredible story."

"Sorry. This coarse word girl is fresh out of ideas," I said.

El Cap nodded, "It requires serious pondering."

"There's nothing we can do, short of destroying the art," Blue said.

"I refuse to let ten thousand-year-old art get destroyed," I shouted.

"Look, we've pondered and debated what-if scenarios since the day we stumbled inside the cave. Each new person who learns of our find puts it one breath closer to global revelation.

When Holly is found, hers will be the breath of destruction," Blue said.

"Don't you mean if she's found? Alive," I said.

El Cap shifted and cleared his throat. "You survived under worse conditions. There's a great chance she may."

"She could be in the cave right now, resting, waiting. It was a refuge for me, she could use it, too."

"Didn't see a bubble or any sign of a diver there," El Cap said.

"We need to dive the cave right away," I said.

Blue stood, "We'll discuss later. First I need to get to the store. El Cap, will you keep Sirena company while I step out for a little?"

"Your avoidance isn't becoming," El Cap quipped.

Blue's face fell slack. "Please enlighten him on the need for me to dash out at this inappropriate moment." When he walked out, the room seemed ten times its size with twice the amount of air.

El Cap's smile turned to a hearty chuckle when he learned of the memory card. His contagious glee infected me with a big laugh, a brief respite from reality. Happy noises fell silent as our smiles diminished. For long minutes we simmered in the heart-wrenching worry of our next step. How to keep our secret safe?

After El Cap hit the shower, he plopped next to me, towel drying his long locks.

"What will we accomplish diving the cave? I think it's best we steer clear of it in case we're being watched."

"Selfish reason, I'd like to shoot more photos and absorb the ambiance before it's obliterated. And…"

El Cap interrupted, "It won't be obliterated."

"Blue's idea is if it's out in the open, then it's gone."

"We'll see. The big if is Holly. If she survives, if she shared the cave art with Aiden. His injury is quite severe."

"Thank God he made it and pray he can't remember shit?"

$-27-$

Day Nine

El Cap threw me a shocked look, resumed drying his hair and then nodded.

"Are you aware Jane and crew left after your homecoming?"

"Yeah. Seems there's a timestamp on Jane's marina environmental piece. Something about airing it before any litigation issues. Plus Jane scored a buyer for the docudrama at sea starring yours truly. Ooh, wish I could get in on the editing process. There's some seriously sick shots of me. In a bad way."

He smiled. "I have a hard time discerning your sarcasm. Both stories should be told and I, for one, am beyond blessed to have you safe and sound."

"Thanks. Don't place any bets on the sound part."

He shot me a hard look.

"Ah, you haven't mentioned how you feel, the healing and all."

"Afraid to speak about it, afraid it'll take a bad turn. Isabelle force feeds me and monitors my water intake. Thankfully she doesn't monitor any output."

He laughed. "Ah, sarcasm."

I shrugged. "Still stiff legged mobility-wise. Sounds crazy but I need a good swim. Doc says time will heal all my flesh wounds. I say a good swim will heal the chaos in my head."

"Not sarcasm," he said and patted my hand. "We have a lot to process, but you have the added burden of knowing someone was or is out to harm you."

"Yeah. I'm safe at the Hideaway. Just thinking of not living in this compound is a scary thing."

"Of course."

"But out on the boat with you and Blue, solid. No qualms. I'm sure of it."

Both of us looked toward the door when we heard it rattle open. Blue let himself in. Walking toward us, he waved a couple of thumb drives. He sat down and got busy making copies and opened up the first of probably hundreds of folders.

"Print it out, I need to hold the paper," I said.

We hunched over the monitor and read typical business letter, saw spreadsheets, nothing of consequence.

He pointed to a bank statement. "Hum. Mary Grace issues through a Cayman account."

El Cap stood and began to pace. "So, we're the only ones to see this?"

"Only us," Blue said.

"Shouldn't the cops get a look at it? I mean, we have two more copies in case it gets lost." I put air quotes around the gets lost part.

After a big pregnant pause El Cap said, "Please don't."

"Why? It gets me off the Inspector's radar and is something he can wag in front of Frick and Frack. Unless he released them, too."

Blue turned to face me. "Timing."

My feet were killing me. I took a seat.

El Cap said, "Who can we trust to make a case with any of this?"

"Good question," said Blue.

"And the hired guns who kidnapped me," I said. Sorry to put Lonnie in a bad position, but dammit Mary Grace needs to pay."

Blue looked me square in the eyes. "She won't wiggle out of this one."

"What makes you so sure?" I couldn't take my eyes off his twinkling baby blues.

"A little birdie told me."

El Cap chuckled and we all bent over laughing. What a magical tonic, laughter.

"I need to rest before supper. Come get me when you find earth shattering evidence."

Blue walked me to my room and helped me find a good place to stash the thumb drive. He hesitated before my door then gave me a kiss on the cheek. "Rest well."

Did I just swoon? Damn, I've already made a fool of myself once over him.

I joined Blue and El Cap for a late supper. Once settled with a cup of tea, I asked, "Are we telling Isabelle?"

Almost simultaneously both men said, "No."

"No what?" Isabelle parroted as she walked up behind us.

"No, we aren't doing shots with Sirena." El Cap said.

Smooth liar, I thought. His quick answer caught me by surprise. Unable to lie or deceive my best friend, I shrugged and laser beamed a look at each of the men.

"You know better than to mix alcohol with the steroids, yes?"

"Yes ma'am." I saluted her.

"Now for the news," Isabelle said and continued, "Holly still missing. Search called off at dark and resume at first light. If the storm allows."

"Storm?" Blue echoed.

"Yes. Coast Guards may have to assist around Bermuda. Seems the storm bounced off the Florida coast and a front is pushing it out to sea."

"How do you know all this?" I was incredulous at the amount of inside info Isabelle could garner. She smiled and sashayed toward a table full of diners.

"Glad my sweet ass didn't have to depend on the eye in the sky to pluck me from the sea."

El Cap whispered, "She may have inside info, but sometimes it isn't the most reliable."

Supper was served and we ate in near silence until I brought up the subject of diving the cave.

El Cap shook his head, "Committed to a morning charter. I'll have to check the manifest, see if Isabelle booked any others. But we could do a night dive."

Blue dropped his fork load of fish. "No."

"Yes," I countered.

"I won't take a chance with your health and we can't afford to dive there and be followed. A night dive on the rocks? Insanity. We may as well erect a flashing buoy."

"Not insanity," El Cap said. "Just cautious."

"Understand precaution. Precisely why it's a no go. And Sirena, don't you get any wise ideas about chartering another boat or going solo."

"Sure. Um, wouldn't Isabelle have mentioned if she booked any other charters? She'd be thrilled to get any boat business on the heels of losing charter revenue from the storm. If not scheduled, you two may want to drum up a few divers. We can join them. Dive in plain sight with the customers. Isn't it your usual MO?"

-28-

Day Ten

Isabelle insisted Rosie room with me. "An unbeatable first alert device," she said. Naturally she waved off the fact I'm afraid of birds and planted his cage in my flat anyway. I protested and said he'd alert to feeding time. She didn't listen to my concerns even when I compared the bird's one-track mind to the current mindset of her baby brother's.

Rosie squawked and rang his bell and otherwise raised hell until I removed the cage cover.

"Good morning, devil bird."

He squawked and cursed his reply "Bitch, bitch, bitch."

"My sweet buoy," I said in my best Bahamian lilt.

He got louder as I headed toward the door. He wanted out. "Bitch, bitch, bitch," I repeated over my shoulder.

His voice was so loud and crystal clear I could understand his words through the door. After locking up, I made my way to Blue's place, only five doors down and knocked. No answer. Banged a little louder and sill no reply.

I slowly took the stairs to the dining hall. Blue and Isabelle were having tea and quiet conversation. We bid our good mornings.

I settled next to them. "What am I interrupting?"

Isabelle rolled her eyes and head toward her brother, a gesture meaning you tell her.

He pointed to a printed spreadsheet labeled contract services.

"These people are on retainer and when they actually work are paid by the job. I'm surmising it's kind of an under the table payment since corporate accounting from MG Enterprises didn't issue these checks. They're issued through a Cayman account."

My stomach tightened all the way to my throat as he read off actual names of the dirty half dozen including the Frick brothers, Refrigerator and Zander.

Blue ran his finger down the page and pointed to Shem Saunders.

"Okay. Who's he?"

He drew in a big breath and let it go. "It's El Cap's given name."

"What the hell?"

Blue nodded. "And something else is a bit strange."

"What might that be?" Isabelle asked.

"Cell phones. Do you pay for El Cap's mobile?"

"Not at all," Isabelle said. "We only use radio. More dependable."

Blue looked up at the ceiling and across to his sister. "I saw two mobiles onboard *Sweet Pea*. Any idea why he'd have two?"

They didn't want to say the obvious so I spelled it out. "One's personal, the other business. Dirty business just like Dragon Lady's other goons."

"Don't call him that," Isabelle snapped.

"Sorry. Blue, you gotta be the one to confront Mr. Shem

the sham. I mean he has to know we're on to him. You told him about finding the memory stick."

"Enough," Isabelle said and rose. "He's like a son to me and until we get his side I shan't stand for any name calling. Do you understand?"

I wanted to call her out on the overt denial. Instead I nodded. "You're right. I was out of line."

Blue stood. "You'll excuse me. Seems I'm destined to conduct some horribly unpleasant business."

Isabelle looked up at her brother and wiped tears away from her weary eyes.

Once Blue was out of the room I took a deep breath and said, "I'm also hurt from the implications about El Cap's, um, activities. But may I change the subject?"

"Please do." She sniffled and sat beside me.

"It's about Zantae. I know she's the one who found me. Wanna know how I know?"

Isabelle was slow to respond to my baited inquiry. "Do tell, gull, since you were delirious and half blind."

"True. Well, two things tipped me off. One. Her voice. Granted we'd only talked briefly over the years. And with my Yankee ears, well, the Bahamian accent could've been anyone." I paused to gauge her reactions.

"Go on." Her tone was neutral and she'd stopped sniffling.

"When she spoke at the clinic, the hairs on my neck raised from the familiar cadence. But like I said, my ears are used to flat American speech. Not the musicality of Biminites."

She smiled and closed her red rimmed eyes.

"My absolute proof is her beauty mark. I touched the face of an angel and felt a little round imperfection under an eye."

"She got one for sure.

"How'd she find me? Hundreds of little islands and sand spits surround Bimini. She came to the very one I washed up on. How? Oh, then, she left as quietly as she arrived. No sounds of motorboats approaching or leaving."

"So many questions. You asking the wrong island girl. Go ask Zantae yourself."

●　●　●

Blue stepped onboard *Sweet Pea*, careful not to fall in the uncovered engine compartment. He watched as El Cap labored in the hot hold. He twisted a wrench around a water pump first one way then the other.

"Down here," he called, "Need a moment to…" his voice trailed off and the sound of metal on metal filled the space. "Ah ha finally got it." He looked up, water pump in one sweaty hand, greasy wrench in the other. "Morning, mate."

"Morning." Blue sat on the rail and stared, "I may have left something down in the cabin. Mind if I give a quick look?"

"Permission granted," he teased.

He returned with the cigar box. "Here it is. Two mobiles," he said with a shrug. "Two. Why?"

El Cap pulled himself out of the engine hole, put the water pump and tool on the deck and then muscled the cover back on. He picked up the wrench and turned it round and round between his dirty hands.

"Why?" He echoed.

Blue perched on the rail. "You're on Mary Grace's deep dark payroll."

El Cap hung his head. "Appears so. There's damning reasoning. Care to hear?

"I'm on the edge of my seat."

~29~

Day Ten

B lue gripped the edge of the rail and leaned forward, his hard gaze pinned on El Cap.

"Yes, of course," El Cap said and added, "Mind if I wash up first?"

Blue stood, waved an arm as in 'be my guest' and followed him inside the cabin. Silence hung between the two like thick hurricane air. El Cap toweled his arms and then reached in the small refrigerator. He tossed a bottle of water to Blue and twisted one open and took a long swig.

"My habit of gaming isn't exactly news. Getting caught up in poker games, losing and telling myself the next hand will put me even. It's what screwed me up."

"Go on."

With a heavy sigh he continued. "Hand after hand, game after game I lost. I'd never had a losing streak like it. My ego got the best of me. I should've stopped." He paced around the cabin.

"Tell me the part about you working for Mary Grace."

He stopped pacing. "She bought my debt from the poker club and waved it under my nose. Said she owned me until I helped her enough to pay it off."

"When the hell did this take place? And why didn't you tell her to take a hike?"

"Almost two years ago. And you know why I had to pony up. You of all people know."

"Don't put this back on me, man."

"Just saying."

"Who tried to kill Sirena?"

Slow and deliberate El Cap raised his shamed head and looked his best friend in the eyes. "I don't know. My moral compass isn't for sale."

"What exactly did you do for Mary Grace, then?"

"Zander flew me and American dollars into Cayman Brac. The hanger manager received a major portion of the payload. While Zander was elsewhere, my job was to stock a home on the island with a list of benign household items."

Blue closed his eyes and leaned his head back. "Mary Grace is hiding out in Cayman."

"Most likely."

"Keep going, as you mentioned, I know this woman and know for a fact you haven't touched the tip of the iceberg yet."

"I helped her get the marina contract."

"How?"

"By reading all her competitors' bids. To, um, insure she got the marina job she submitted three percent below the lowest bidder. She was awarded and my debt was this close to being over." He held up a thumb and forefinger showing a small measurement.

"And the blast?"

"I had nothing to do with the blast. I'd die myself before killing our reefs. Or anybody, especially Sirena. Damn, man, give me a little credit here."

"Yeah, credit. You sure got credit with the Dragon Lady," Blue shook his head in disgust.

"Before you dismiss me as a traitor, hear me out. Someone ordered another blast to purge coral from a particularly stubborn spot in the canal. Frick and Frack planted the explosives."

"Live explosives ready to kill any moment? Damn man." Blue's jaw muscled jumped and he leaned in close to El Cap's sweat beaded face.

El Cap backed away. "Hell. No. I was an errand at the marina office and spotted Zander take a paper bag from some white guy and walk into the employee locker room. In no time he came back out and took off, no bag. So I went in there, opened up lockers and found it. A neat little explosive packet. I took out the putty and stuck wadded up paper in its place." Frick and Frack are so dumb they wouldn't know the difference. Even if they did, they'd never speak up."

"Brave act, grave consequences," Blue said in a whisper.

"Seemed right at the time.

"Redemption."

"Yeah. Let me finish. Ten minutes later Zander was back with Frick and Frack in tow."

"You're saying Mary Grace set all this in motion?"

El Cap shrugged. "No proof whatsoever."

● ● ●

Zantae called Church Sister. "Hey Sister, still got yo' little skiff?"

"You know I do. Why?"

"Any chance I can borrow it?"

"Well, yeah, send someone over to get it. What you need it for?"

"Never you mind."

"Woman, you crazy."

"Beside the point. Fill her up, I'll pay you for the petrol. When I come for it, I'll leave cash under the big ole conch shell on your porch. Trust me, your little boat okay wid me."

"I must be crazy as you. It'll be settin' on ready."

● ● ●

Day Eleven

Starlight and moon beams highlighted Zantae's sweat beaded skin and danced off the slow moving skiff. A twist of the throttle silenced the outboard's steady drone.

Midnight. She secured the bobbing vessel to the mooring ball closest to Bimini Rocks. Waves splashed cadence along the weathered hull. Cloudless, the clear sky channeled heavenly light across Zantae. She wore a cape adorned with fish scales. A gusty breeze lifted the thin fabric tied across her square, brown shoulders.

Dipping both hands in the water excited green phosphorescence. Thrusting arms skyward, the illuminated water tinted her skin. Head back, face peering skyward, she sang in a melodic but unusual language.

Perched on the skinny wood bench she rhythmically swayed to her song's ethereal beat. Leaning overboard she stuck her arms in the sea, all the way to her shoulders. Like a child at play, she swirled her arms back and forth, back and forth, serenading the sea.

Her siren's song quieted to a hum as she pulled her arms from the water, sat back and unfolded her long legs. She untied the cape, letting it pool across her bare feet. Fish scales tattooed her shimmering skin. One giant stride dropped her into the calm sea.

A trail of green traced her plunge. Feet first she landed on the coral chimney protrusion. A hint of starlight caressed her silhouette. She found a sitting spot and dangled her legs over the chimney. As her legs rose up, they melded into one long appendage.

Zantae pushed off and with dolphin stealth dived toward the seafloor. Undulating kicks transported her beneath the cavernous overhang. Arms thrust forward, back arched, her powerful tail propelled her up. Eager hands tapped along the roof of the cavern until she found the opening. In a flash she rocketed inside.

Treading water in the dark abyss, she violently sucked air, close to hyperventilation. Heart steady and breath returned to a manageable level, she released the tension in her neck and shoulders.

Wham, a hard gut punch knocked the air out of her. She flew backward and went under. Breaking the surface, she coughed and spit on her return to the world of air. Arms wrapped around her upper torso for protection, she twisted around and called out, "Show yourself, you coward."

Cursing her tympanic heart, she slowly reached out and felt across the face of the water. She hit a hard surface and drew back.

"Hard shell, whew, not a shark." Her words echoed in the chamber.

Tap, tap, tap she moved her hands around the hefty, barnacle-riddled creature. Sucking in courage with inhalations.

"You devil. Anybody else and I may be drawin' back a nub. So this is your lair. Well, One Eye, you're fixin' to get evicted."

Gentle, firm hands pushed his shell. "Go on, now."

Her touches ignited the glow across his mighty shell. She watched him drop to the exit door.

Drawing in an exaggerated breath until she could hold no more, Zantae followed the same path as One Eye. As soon as she was on the other side of the hidden cave entrance, she expelled her breath hard enough for phosphorescence to come alive. Hands propped on either side of the exit, she drew back and forcefully expelled her air supply back and forth across the opening. A membrane like a wobbly bubble formed then thickened.

One swift tail kick propelled her to the surface. She floated on her back, gasping for air.

-30-

Day Eleven

Daylight painted the sky and the sun wasted little time in heating the humid summer air. A clock at Isabelle's bedside chimed seven and the phone rang simultaneously. She threw back the covers, peeked at the time and reached for the land line.

"No rest for the weary," she muttered.

"Hey. It's me, Church Sistah. Have you seen Zantae? "

"Uh you mean right now? I've not had my tea, much less a chat with her or anyone else for that matter. Why?"

"Worried. She borrowed my boat and hasn't come back yet. Well. The boat's not back and she's not answering the radio."

Awake and in need of her morning cup, Isabelle replied, "She took out your homemade wood skiff with the outboard what could be in a museum? You lost your mind?"

"Don't scold me. She's the one took it out. Besides if I said no, she'd have taken it anyway."

Isabelle sighed. "Radio right away if, when she shows up. Let me get dressed and see what I can do."

• • •

A week later

The evening before El Cap went to Nassau to give depositions and offer testimony regarding MG Enterprises, unexpected visitors knocked on his door.

"What a nice surprise. Please come in." Closing the door, a puzzled look crossed his face.

Blue shook his hand and gave him a bro hug. Then Lonnie put her slender arms around El Cap and hugged him tight.

"Charter's not the same without you." She shrugged. "The Captain Auntie hired is okay but...I miss you."

"I'll be back in a few weeks then I get to boss you around, yes?"

They all laughed and El Cap motioned for them to sit.

Blue spoke first. "Well, tourism's alive and well again. Seems the Hideaway could serve as the Minister of Tourism's poster child."

El Cap raised an eyebrow. "Brilliant. But I'm sure you didn't come all the way up here to give me a business report."

Looking at his daughter, he cocked his head to the side. She cleared her throat.

"There's something you must have before you go to Nassau." She reached inside her cross body purse, dug around a bit and then handed him a small packet.

He studied the packet. "Oh, what's this?"

Blue said, "Open it."

He slid a finger under the taped paper and out tumbled a photo memory card. He held it up and said, "More MG accounting?"

Blue shook his head.

Lonnie slowly choked out her words. "Images Papa and Sirena took of the blast site. I should've given them to you sooner. I was really mad at you for working with Mother Mary Grace. I felt betrayed. Please accept my apology."

El Cap nodded. "Apology not necessary. I should ask for your forgiveness. And thank you, this could be the key to our case. You're a real hero, Lanky Lonnie."

Blue put an arm around his daughter and then wiped her tears. "Something else, you should know, El Cap. The good lieutenant hinted to a little cheating going on at the poker tables, specifically aimed at you."

El Cap caught the implications. "Dragon Lady set me up."

"Appears so. When I let Lonnie in on the possible cheating, she saw the predicament you were put in and did the right thing by you."

"I need to take back something, then." El Cap said and added, "You're not only my hero, you're Bimini's hero."

● ● ●

Zantae heard a knock at her front door. "Sirena?"

"Yes ma'am, it's me."

"Then come in, it's unlocked."

I juggled an armload of grocery bags and managed to let myself in.

"More care packages from Isabelle?"

"Yep. She shows her love through food, you know."

"Yeah, is good to be loved."

I plopped the bags on the kitchen table and refrigerated the cool items. Putting stuff on the herb shelf, clumsy me knocked something over. Setting it upright, my fingers froze on a familiar object.

Right about then, Zantae sung out, "Come on in here. I'll do that later. Sit with me."

The little drinking vessel and I went into the sitting room. I plopped next to her.

"So, you look better. Feeling good?"

I nodded and put the cup in her hand. "Look what I found."

She examined it. "Huh, you giving me an empty cup. I could use a little tea in here."

"Or you could serve me some honey water. Like the kind you plied me with on the islet."

"All right then. We'll get to that later. First thing, you went back to the art cave, yes?

"Serious?"

"Humor yo elder. We'll get to other tings next."

I gave her a nod of incredulity.

"Tell me what you know."

I shrugged. "It's gone."

She gave my hand a couple of little squeezes like a secret consent.

"You knew it wouldn't be there, the entrance," I said and added, "just like you knew where to find me."

"What make you so sure?"

"You aren't denying it."

Feather soft, I glided a finger over her beauty mark and then thumped the tin cup in her hand. "One just like this was on the islet with me. You brought it there."

"Huh."

"Uh-huh. So how'd you do it?"

"Do what?"

"We'll start with how you found me and we'll take it from there."

"I got a gift and I used it. Simple."

"Yeah, I get the telecommunication part of the gift. Explain teleportation."

"Who says teleport? I didn't say teleport."

"We're playing verbal volley ball, Miss Zantae. And so far, you've scored all the points. I'm gonna spike one over to ya. How'd your sweet ass end up on the islet? No boat. You surely didn't parasail in."

"You always sass yo elders?"

"No ma'am, I'm totally exasperated."

Resting her head on the sofa back, Zantae closed her eyes and let out a long sigh.

"Why'd you latch onto Bimini and Atlantis and not let go? So many others pokin' 'round the rocks. But you the one to find the lost link. They a reason."

"Me? I got some powerful wisdom handed down. But all you got to say is a dream told you. Huh. Way mo' to it." She rolled her head side-to-side then sat forward and looked right at me.

"One day I gonna pass the wisdom on. Might even be sassy pants you. But lemme be clear. Today ain't the day."

THE END

Made in the USA
Columbia, SC
01 July 2021

41255107R00131